Last Laugh

Last Laugh

K. R. Alexander

Scholastic Inc.

Copyright © 2024 by Alex R. Kahler writing as K. R. Alexander

ISBN 978-1-339-01215-5

10 9 8 7 6 5 4 3 2 1   24 25 26 27 28

Printed in the U.S.A.   40

First printing 2024

Book design by Maeve Norton

FOR THE PRACTICAL JOKERS

O

If you asked your friends to list five things they're scared of, I can almost guarantee that one of them will be clowns. There's even a word for it, *coulrophobia*, because I guess so many people are scared of clowns that science had to make it a *thing*.

I don't know why. Maybe it's the garishly painted faces . . . or the eyes that always seem to be staring into your soul. Maybe it's the cackling laugh . . . or the fact that they're always smiling, no matter how sad or scary the situation is.

Heck, maybe it's the big shoes.

The point is, I never understood it before.

To me, clowns were just *silly*. Adults walking around in ridiculous costumes, with clothes that don't fit and really bad makeup and even worse jokes? What's scary about that?

Yeah.

That was before.

Before, when my top five fears were completely

rational: The dark. Heights. Caves. Spiders. And that split second when you look in the bathroom mirror, right as you flick on the light, and worry you'll see someone standing behind you.

Before, when I still thought bravery meant doing things you were told *not* to do.

Before, when the secrets of my grandma's bedroom were still, well, secret.

But then I decided to be the clown.

I went into the room.

I stole what I never should have taken.

And now, no matter how many times I try to give that terrible clown doll back, I can't make it go away.

I can't make any of them go away.

There are so many of them.

Everywhere.

Following me.

Haunting me.

Hunting me.

And if I don't find a way to get rid of them, the final joke is going to be on me.

1

"Victor, get in here and help your sister with her homework!"

My mom's voice echoes through our apartment, piercing even my noise-canceling headphones. I pause my game and pull them down around my neck.

"What?" I call out. Even though I heard her the first time. I just know the question gets under her skin. Almost as much as being forced to help my little sister, Genevieve, gets under mine.

I hear Mom groan from the kitchen.

"I said, come and help your little sister with her homework!"

I mutter to myself as I set the controller down and get out of my beanbag chair. I'm half tempted to keep playing. Then when Mom eventually comes in and demands to know why I didn't help, I'll coolly reply that *she didn't say the magic word*.

Or not. Even though I like being right, I don't like being grounded. So. Here we go.

I make my way to the living room, where Genevieve is sitting at the coffee table with her books and papers spread out in a mess before her.

Genevieve is like my complete opposite. And also the complete opposite of my older sister, Sarah. While Sarah and I are funny and adventurous and really not that into school, Genevieve is a total nerd. She's super quiet and shy and doesn't have many friends. She's eight, four years younger than me. Sarah's sixteen.

Genevieve does *not* need my help. I think this is just my mom's way of keeping me from playing video games. Especially since we don't even have school tomorrow—it's a teacher workshop day.

"What's the damage, twerp?" I ask, sitting across the table from Genevieve.

"Math," she replies. "And I'm not a twerp."

"Could've fooled me."

She sticks out her tongue, but she doesn't say anything else. Also unlike me, she's a complete pushover.

She's got curly black hair and dark olive skin, just like me and Sarah. But whereas I'm tall and keep my hair cut close, Genevieve is short, and her hair nearly reaches her midback. I lean over and start helping her work. As expected, she's already half done with her homework, but she doesn't mind the extra hand.

The one thing that my siblings and I have in

common? We're all really smart. Genevieve's just the only one who seems proud of it.

So I help her with her homework while she does most of the work and my mom finishes up dinner. Dad normally cooks, but he works Thursday nights. Sarah is . . . well, I have no idea where Sarah is. Like usual.

Mom has me set the table, and she's just putting out a giant pot of pasta when the front door opens and Sarah walks in.

Sarah has streaks of blue and green in her long curls, and her clothes are mismatched in a way that totally makes sense. But it's not how she looks that makes her cool—it's how she acts. When she walks into a room, she owns it. No matter where she is, she acts like she's the hero of the story. Which makes the rest of us her sidekicks, I guess.

She tosses her backpack on the sofa and tousles my hair.

"How's the homework, twerp?" she asks Genevieve.

I snicker. She totally stole the word from me, and I love how much it bugs Genevieve.

"Done," Genevieve replies. She glares at Sarah. "No thanks to you."

"Ouch! I'm slain!" Sarah says with a dramatic flop to the couch.

Genevieve giggles, dropping her angry front, and jumps on top of Sarah, tickling her relentlessly.

Like I said, total pushover.

"Come on, you three," Mom says from the dining room. "Time to eat."

We head into the dining room and settle in.

Our condo isn't huge, but it's ours. Even without Dad here tonight there's just barely enough room for us at the table. We pile in, and Sarah begins shoveling food onto her plate before Mom has even set out the salad.

"Leave some for the rest of us!" Mom yelps.

Sarah chuckles, takes another small scoop, and passes the tongs to me. I make sure to serve Genevieve first before I pile up the noodles on my own plate. I'm her big brother. Even if we get on each other's nerves, I gotta take care of her.

Mom asks us about our days, and I sort of tune it out, already thinking about the upgrades I need to make to my avatar in the game. I hear Genevieve mention some kids at school who made fun of her—I know Sarah's gonna talk to her about that later, because Sarah is the type who just refuses to be picked on—and Sarah mentions some extra band practice coming up. I even manage to talk about what we were doing in science class today even though I'm not really paying attention. Hopefully it sounds at least a little smart.

Then Mom says something that makes me focus in.

At least, to the second part of the sentence.

"—Grandma's for the long weekend."

"What?" I ask.

"I'm taking Grandma out to Iowa City this weekend for some scans. Totally routine," Mom says. "So you three are going to stay there to take care of her cats tomorrow night."

"But I have band practice!" Sarah interjects.

"And we're too young to take care of the cats," Genevieve sagely says.

"You'll be fine," Mom tells her. There's a tired look in her eyes that begs us not to push it. "Your dad will be there for bedtime, but he's working tomorrow night so you'll have to feed the cats dinner. That's it. It's just one night."

"But I'm allergic," I say.

I'm not, really. But I also really don't want to go over there. Grandma somehow doesn't have the internet, our phone plan won't let me stream games, and I'm supposed to raid a dungeon with some friends.

I mean, sometimes I sneeze a little bit at Grandma's place, but that could also be the dust.

"Please," Mom says. It's not a request or a question. "You know I wouldn't ask if it wasn't important."

"Are we getting paid?" Sarah asks.

"Paid?" Mom replies.

"Well, yeah. We should be getting paid for catsitting."

Mom lets out a big sigh.

"I'll take you out for ice cream after. Okay? Just do this for me? This once?"

"We will, Mom," Genevieve answers for us.

I look at Sarah, and Sarah looks at me. *Total pushover.* But there's also no point in arguing.

"Thank you," Mom says. "It'll be over before you know it."

If only I'd known how terribly wrong she was.

2

The next day, Sarah and Genevieve and Mom and I are standing outside the door to Grandma's house. My sisters and I have our overnight bags packed—me with just a change of clothes and some chargers and a book, Sarah looking like she's packed for a month abroad. Genevieve is wearing the unicorn backpack she takes to school. I helped her pack to make sure she had everything. Of course, there was no need— *she* was the one reminding *me* to pack a spare phone charger.

"Do we really have to do this?" Sarah groans under her breath.

Mom nudges her. "Be nice."

Sarah just grumbles.

Then the door opens, and whatever glum expression Sarah had is replaced by a huge smile. All of us smile the moment Grandma opens the door. It's hard not to.

She's got wispy salt-and-pepper hair and walks

with a cane from an old ballet accident, but she's as energetic as a puppy. The moment she sees us, she wraps us all up in a big hug.

"You're all getting so big!" she says. "I'm going to have to get a stepladder to hug you soon. Come in, come in! It's cold outside."

She gestures us in, and my mom and sisters step in. I hesitate.

From the outside, Grandma's house looks like any other house. A single-story box with a big yard, just like the dozen other houses on the street. The paint is a chipped and fading shade of mustard. The yard is overgrown because Dad hasn't come over to mow for a while—too many late nights running the restaurant. But everything is still tidy. Normal. You wouldn't look at it twice.

Inside is a completely different story.

And look—I'm not ashamed to admit it:

The place kinda freaks me out.

I take a deep breath and step in, closing the door behind me.

It's like stepping into a very strange and very cluttered museum.

Every inch of space on the walls is covered in paintings or masks or old Victorian portraits—you can't even see if there's paint or wallpaper behind them.

Shelves are laden with everything from porcelain ballerina music boxes to wooden marionettes to antique Venetian masks. There are stands teetering with old books and figurines along the walls, and intricate mobiles and grand chandeliers hanging from the ceiling. There are also stranger things, *darker* things, like skulls from enormous cats, perfectly preserved fish skeletons, and even a taxidermy monkey.

It isn't exactly a hoarder's house, but it isn't exactly *not* a hoarder's house. It's all arranged and carefully dusted.

When my grandpa died, long before I was born, Grandma was inspired from her years on the road doing ballet to travel again. So she did. She took the money Grandpa left her and traveled the globe, collecting hundreds of strange artifacts along the way. There's so much here that she could probably charge admission. I don't know how she keeps track of all of it, but she does—she knows where everything is kept. She's also very strict about moving things around.

Sarah once switched two glass horse figurines on the shelf, and Grandma noticed immediately. Grandma's a really nice woman, but I'd never seen her so angry and disappointed before. She kept saying that Sarah could have hurt herself fooling around with things like that, before making us all go to bed without any TV. The three of us had lain awake in the spare bedroom, whispering and wondering how in the world Sarah could have hurt herself on a glass figurine. Maybe if it had broken, sure, but Grandma had acted like Sarah was playing with matches by a gas can.

Weirdly, none of Grandma's cats seem to bother the artifacts. My friend Gareth thinks she's trained them.

"You're sure you're okay leaving us in charge?" Sarah asks when we're all in Grandma's living room. Grandma has her day bag packed and waiting by the door—it's clear she's been ready to go for a while. It's also clear that Sarah remembers getting scolded by Grandma.

Grandma doesn't answer right away. Her gaze takes in each of us in turn. When her eyes land on me, they linger.

A chill races down my back.

"I'm sure," she finally says. "You know the rules."

I can't help it—I look down the hall the moment she says it. At the far end is a closed door.

I've never been in there. None of us have.

I've barely even seen it open.

Grandma's rules are simple and concrete:

> *Don't touch anything.*
> *Don't stay up too late.*
> *And don't go into my bedroom.*

Honestly, they're pretty much the same rules we have at home. Minus the not-touching-anything part, because that would just be strange. But every time she mentions them, that chill trickles down my spine.

Normally, when adults make rules, it feels like they're doing it to keep kids out of their hair, to keep them out of trouble.

But Grandma's rules, well . . .

the way she says them makes me feel like they're the only things keeping us safe.

3

Mom and Grandma don't linger—Mom gets super anxious about driving to the city, especially when she's worried she'll hit rush hour traffic. Knowing her, they'll arrive five hours early and spend the afternoon in the hospital cafeteria.

"What do you twerps want for lunch?" Sarah asks.

"Peanut butter and jelly!" Genevieve calls out.

"A T-bone steak and mashed potatoes," I say.

"Yes to you," Sarah says to Genevieve, "and definite no to you," she says, pointing to me. "You get PB and J too."

"I thought you wanted to be a chef like Dad one day?" I ask, settling in at the kitchen table. Even the table is covered in oddities—a giant metal birdcage sits in the center, stuffed with doll heads and peacock feathers.

"I do," Sarah replies. "But that doesn't mean I want to create amazing meals for people who won't appreciate them. You probably want your steak well-done and served with ketchup."

"What's wrong with that?" I ask.

"Everything," she replies.

"I'd like my PB and J rare," Genevieve says. She sits down at the table beside me and sticks out her tongue. I stick mine out in response.

Sarah starts playing some music on her phone, and Genevieve pulls out her book, so I pull out my phone and start texting Gareth. It feels strange being in here without any adults.

Sarah's watched us dozens of times, but that's always been at home. Here, it feels weird. Emptier. But also somehow not.

Almost like all the antiques along the walls are watching us. Waiting.

I think that's why Sarah has the music up so loud. It makes the room feel less . . . expectant.

"Here you go," Sarah says when she sets the sandwiches down. She made one for herself as well, and leans back against the counter to eat it. "Bon appétit. And if you think you can do better, Victor, today's your chance. I'm going to be leaving in a few hours, so dinner is all on you."

"What?" Genevieve and I ask in unison. Sarah

says it so casually, like it's no big deal, even though it *is* a big deal. I mean, I'm old enough to watch Genevieve for a few hours, but *in this house*? Just the thought makes me shudder.

Genevieve continues. "You can't leave us all alone." She almost whimpers when she says it, which makes me just a little offended—I mean, *I'm* here.

"It's just for a little while," Sarah says. "I'll be back before Dad gets off work. I can't miss band practice."

"So practice tomorrow," Genevieve whines.

"No go, twerp. Alex will break up with me if I skip—we've got a show coming up." Sarah comes over and sits on the opposite side of the table. "Victor's gonna be in charge while I'm gone."

I don't know where the words come from, but before I can stop myself I say, "But Mom and Grandma will be mad at you."

Ugh, it sounds like something Genevieve would say.

Sarah leans in. There's a glint in her eyes that makes me swallow hard. Sarah is always the laughing, silly one. But her look is deadly serious.

"Not if neither of you tells them," she says. She looks point-blank at me. "Don't be a baby, Victor. You always say you want to be treated like a grown-up, so act like one. Unless you're too scared of a repeat of last time?" She rattles the cage in the center of the table at that, making the doll heads within clatter. I swear half of them turn to face me in that motion, their blank glass eyes locked on mine.

I turn away and look at Sarah instead. Anger boils in my chest. It takes a lot to get me angry, but she knows exactly what to say.

I'm not a baby. I'm not scared of an empty house.

Except she knows I am.

She knows, because two years ago, Sarah and I stayed here overnight. I'd been terrified of the creepy statues in the room, and the sound of the cats rustling around in the darkness.

At one point in the night, I woke up to go to the bathroom.

When I got back, there was a doll sitting on my pillow.

I screamed so loud I think the neighbors heard it.

This made Sarah burst out laughing.

Grandma had been so mad at Sarah that night, I was actually afraid of her. Sarah wasn't allowed back in the house for *months*.

But Sarah thought it was worth it. She's tormented me about it ever since.

"I'm not a baby," I say, my teeth clenched.

"Good. Then prove it."

"I will," I reply.

My eyes flicker to Grandma's closed bedroom door.

I know precisely how I'm going to do it.

4

Sarah leaves shortly after lunch.

She says she'll only be gone two or three hours, and I know she'll stick to that—she doesn't want to get in trouble, and if Dad gets here before she's back, she'll be grounded for a month.

Which means it's just me and Genevieve and Grandma's three cats—Tibbits, Yellow, and Marcy. The five of us sit in the living room. Grandma has a TV, but she doesn't have internet or cable, so we have an old DVD of *Monsters, Inc.* we've both seen a hundred times playing in the background. Genevieve is too busy reading a book to watch, and I'm too busy playing a game on my phone to care. But the background noise is nice.

Otherwise, it's way too easy to become aware of the heavy silence of the house. The terrifying sensation of all the strange dolls and sculptures and taxidermy staring at us. My eyes flick up to see a porcelain marionette on the top of a bookshelf leaning precariously over the edge, its black eyes directed at me.

I love my grandma but, man, this place creeps me out.

I just have to hope it creeps Sarah out as much.

I have to scare her. And it has to be a good scare. Something she'd never see coming, something she'd never *want* to see coming. And there's one thing in this world that scares her more than anything else.

Clowns.

It's like a gut-deep fear. When you see movies or cartoons where someone leaps on a chair screaming because there's a mouse scurrying around? That's my big sister with clowns. We once found her hiding in the back seat of our car at a theme park because she'd seen a clown by the Tilt-A-Whirl. She's left movies if a clown appears onscreen, even if it's a comedy and the clown is, like, some kid's birthday party entertainer.

I once got her a birthday card with a clown on it as a joke.

She tore it up, shoved it down the garbage disposal, and wouldn't talk to me for three weeks.

The trouble is, for all the creepy knickknacks Grandma has around the house, she doesn't have any clowns. At least, none out here.

But I know she has some.

Once, when we were sleeping over, I was leaving the guest room the same time Grandma was leaving her bedroom, and I saw past her, just for a moment, just before she shut the door.

And there,

on her nightstand,

was a porcelain clown doll.

I didn't see much more—Grandma shut the door behind her immediately and I pretended not to have seen a thing. I never investigated further. I assume she keeps them back there because Sarah's so deathly afraid of them.

Grandma's really kind and caring like that.

Sarah doesn't know there's a clown doll in Grandma's bedroom. If she did, she'd never step foot in Grandma's house again.

All of this is perfect for me.

After I'm *positive* Sarah has made it to band practice and won't be coming back to grab something she forgot, I set down my phone.

"Bathroom break," I say for absolutely no reason, and then realize it's probably more suspicious than if I'd said nothing.

Genevieve just grunts and continues reading. I stand up and make my way down the hall, trying not to trip over any of the cats. I head to the bathroom and open the door, but I don't step inside. Instead, I turn on the faucet so Genevieve can hear water running, close the door, and tiptoe down to Grandma's room.

My heart hammers in my chest and my hands shake, just a little. I might not follow all the rules all the time, but this feels wrong on a very deep level. I don't know why, but it feels more dangerous than the time Gareth convinced me to pet Ms. Jameson's pet Rottweiler.

Scooby ended up being really nice, but I have a feeling whatever is in here will be anything but.

I grab the handle and turn . . .

"What are you doing?"

I nearly jump out of my skin as I spin around to see Genevieve standing in the hall, book in hand and an accusing look on her face.

"What are *you* doing?" I ask back.

"You said you were going to the bathroom," she says.

"Yeah, so why are you out here watching me?"

"I'm not. But you turned the water on immediately, so I knew something was up. You're really bad at being subtle."

I don't know who taught her the word *subtle*, but I hate them.

"I'm—" I begin, but I don't know how to finish the sentence. *Lost?*

"You're not supposed to go in there," she says.

"I know, but . . ." I search for words. "Sarah shouldn't have left us. And she shouldn't have called me a baby. I'm just getting her back."

"By breaking Grandma's rules?"

"No," I say. "By scaring Sarah."

This gets her attention. We both love Sarah, but we also both love scaring her. That's what siblings are for, right? One time while Sarah was babysitting, Genevieve and I devised an elaborate prank where we pretended she'd gotten her hand sawn off. Genevieve came in with a ketchup-covered towel wrapped over her hand, crying at full volume. *We* thought it was hilarious, but Sarah did not. And neither did our parents when she told them what happened.

We got grounded, and Sarah got a new phone case.

"How are you going to scare her?" Genevieve asks me now.

"Clowns," I reply. And before she can talk me out of it, I open Grandma's door.

Genevieve gasps.

When I peer into the room, I gasp too.

5

When I got that one previous magical glimpse into Grandma's bedroom, I saw a single clown on her nightstand. In my head, that's all I assumed there was.

One clown, one easy scare.

I was very,

very

wrong.

There isn't a single clown in the bedroom.

There are

h u n d r e d s.

I step into the room, my mouth hanging open, and Genevieve nudges in beside me, her book completely forgotten.

"How many are there?" she whispers in awe.

"I don't even know," I reply in a similar tone.

They are everywhere.

A dozen plush and knit clown dolls pile atop Grandma's bed, their button eyes staring lifelessly at us. Her nightstand is covered in tiny clown figurines—all shapes and ages, some smiling and others frowning, in every color and pattern of clothing you can imagine. Porcelain-and-fabric dolls lounge on her windowpane, their long arms and legs trailing toward the carpet. One entire wall is a shelf that bows under the weight of even more clowns: translucent glass clowns with bubble-like heads and hair, bobblehead clowns with glassy tears, tiny pewter figurines, marionettes with red noses. There's even a stuffed teddy bear with clown makeup and a big striped bow.

"This is so disturbing," Genevieve says.

Again with the big vocabulary.

"I was gonna say 'weird,' but yeah."

I had no idea Grandma had such a fascination with clowns. She's never brought them up, never tried to get us to go to the circus, never hired one for our birthdays. She's never mentioned them, not once. Not unless it was in relation to Sarah's fear of them, at least.

So the fact that she loves them so much is . . . a surprise.

A *disturbing* surprise.

It feels like secret information, and I don't know what to do with that.

Do our parents know about this?

Does anybody?

"Which one are you going to pick to scare Sarah?" Genevieve asks.

I look around.

Honestly? Now that I'm here and looking at them, I don't *want* to pick any of them. I'm not scared by them—mostly just weirded out—but there's something unsettling about this room. The hairs on my forearms are prickling up, and I have the strongest sensation

> I'm
> being
> watched.

And that strange sensation is coming from all over. From every beady,

> glassy,
> or button
> eye.

The clowns are watching me. I know it.

Get ahold of yourself! I think. *They're just toys. Creepy toys.*

There's a clown over in the corner that catches my attention. It's almost hidden in a pile of other clowns on the floor. Easy to miss, in case Grandma comes back early for some reason. It's not that big—smaller than the teddy bear. It has a white porcelain head and giant red lips, while its body is a striped satin suit. Its white gloved hands are splayed wide, as if waving hello, and its feet are wearing giant red shoes.

Always the stupid big shoes, I think.

I slip around to the other side of the bed—for some reason, it feels like I need to be quiet—and stand before it.

"Careful," Genevieve whispers.

"It's just—" I begin. But I can't finish the sentence. I want to say *It's just a toy* but . . . I don't know. For some reason that feels like a lie.

I look back down to the clown at my feet. It stares across the room blankly. My heart hammers.

Don't be a baby. You can do this. Just pick it up.

I slowly

    crouch

        down

and just as my hand reaches for the doll, something behind me

    CRASHES.

I leap up and look back.

Tibbits dashes off down the hall. The stupid cat knocked over one of Grandma's vases in the hallway. From here, I can see the spilled fake flowers, but it looks like the vase itself isn't broken.

"I'll get it," Genevieve says. She darts out and begins putting the flowers back. Clearly, she doesn't want to be in the room anymore, because she hates cleaning.

Strange, I think. *Grandma's cats usually know better . . .*

Before I can start second-guessing, I reach down and pick up the clown doll. It's cold, and the satin is soft under my hand.

"You're not that scary, are you?" I ask it.

The clown does nothing.

Of *course* it does nothing—it's a *doll.*

I turn and leave Grandma's bedroom, giving one last quick glance around to make sure everything else is still in its proper place.

Everything is.

At least, I think it is.

It must be my imagination—are some of the dolls watching me? And wasn't that porcelain one over there crying a moment before? Now, it's smiling.

"Get ahold of yourself," I whisper to myself. "You're supposed to be scaring Sarah, not yourself."

I shut the door behind me and head back into the guest room.

There's a bed and two cots. Sarah claimed the bed, of course. *Older sister privilege,* she said. So I go over and pull back the covers and hide the clown right below the pillow, so when I pull the covers back over she won't notice a thing.

"She'll never know what hit her," I say with a grin.

Then I turn out the lights and head back to the living room to wait for Sarah to return.

6

Sarah returns less than two hours later.

"How was practice?" I ask as innocently as I can.

"Fine," she replies. "We're playing at the Dark Note next week, and Alex wants us to have everything memorized by then. Like *that* will happen."

The Dark Note is our town's only café. They host open mics for all ages on Friday nights, so even though it won't be, like, their show, it's also the first time they will have performed anywhere other than Alex's garage.

"You can do it if you apply yourself," Genevieve says from her spot on the sofa.

Eesh, does she read motivational posters in her free time?

"Thanks, twerp."

Genevieve rolls her eyes.

"I'm gonna grab a snack in the kitchen," Sarah says. "Anyone want anything?"

"Cotton candy pizza!"

"Unicorn hot dogs."

"Ugh, I don't even know why I ask," Sarah groans.

Sarah heads into the kitchen and I go back to playing my game, wishing it was bedtime for the first time in my life because pretending that I'm not waiting for Sarah to pull back the covers and scream is harder than I expected.

That's why, when Sarah yelps from the kitchen, the only thing I can think of is: *Is it the clown?* Which is stupid, because obviously not.

"What is it?" I ask.

Genevieve and I stand up and go into the kitchen to see Sarah standing over the sink, one hand to her mouth.

"Which one of you did this?" Sarah asks.

She looks at me accusingly, because Genevieve is basically the family angel.

"What are you talking about?"

"This!"

She points into the sink.

My gut gives a lurch as I walk over and look inside.

There, half shoved down the garbage disposal, are the clothes that Sarah brought over. Her T-shirt pokes up from the drain and wet socks hang off the spout. At first, I think they're covered in blood. Then I realize . . .

"Really?" Sarah demands. "Ketchup? Again? Grow up, Victor."

With an angry sigh she yanks her clothes from the drain and begins washing the ketchup off with soap and water.

"At least you were *nice* enough not to turn on the garbage disposal," Sarah says gruffly.

"I didn't do it," I finally say.

"Right," she replies. "Who did? The cats?"

"It wasn't me!" I insist.

"It wasn't me either," Genevieve says.

"I know it wasn't you, twerp." Sarah glares at me. "Now I have to go back home to get clean clothes. And *you're* going to be the one to tell Dad why I have to leave during dinner."

I look to the clock on the wall. Dad won't be here for at least half an hour.

"Can't you go now?" I ask.

"And leave you alone again? Heck no!"

She wrings out her clothes and drapes them over the faucet. "Was this your payback for me leaving?"

"No," I say. "I didn't—"

"What, then? Some sort of joke? Well, I'm not laughing, Victor. Grow. Up." She looks at me for a moment. "You know what? Mom put me in charge. And I think you need to go to your room."

It's so ridiculous I almost laugh. *Sarah? Punishing me? After she literally just broke the rules by leaving?*

But her glare stops that laugh in my throat.

"I didn't do it," I manage to whisper.

"Then who did?" she presses.

It's such an innocent question. It should be easy to answer. But I have no clue. I was with Genevieve all day, and unless the cats have somehow developed opposable thumbs and the ability to open the refrigerator, there are no other suspects. The front door's been locked this whole time.

"Maybe the house is haunted," Genevieve peeps up.

I actually jump a bit. I forgot she was still standing there.

"Very funny," Sarah replies. She points to the hallway. "Room. Now. You can come out when Dad is home."

I grumble under my breath and tromp to the room, shutting the door behind me. I don't know what's worse—being in trouble for something I didn't do, or not knowing how in the world the clothes got in there. It just shouldn't be possible.

The room feels cold. Colder than before. But it's probably my imagination.

I sit down on my cot, pull out my phone, and start

to text Gareth to complain about how unfair this all is.

Then I pause.

I look up at the guest bed. A terrible idea forms as I stare at the spot where I hid the clown. But . . . hadn't I tucked the covers in better than that?

No.

It couldn't have been.

Could it?

I set the phone down and stand, trying to ignore the fact that my legs and hands are shaking.

Carefully, as though there might be a live snake under there, I pull

back

the comforter.

I don't realize I'm holding my breath until I let it out in relief.

The clown is still there. Hiding. Just where I left it.

Of course it is.

"Get ahold of yourself," I whisper.

I tuck the clown back under the covers and smooth them out so no one will notice a thing, then flop back down on my cot and text my friend.

But even then, I can't focus.

All I can think about are Sarah's sodden clothes, and who put them there.

I look up to the numerous figurines and statues filling the room. Almost all of them seem to be watching me.

It makes me wonder if Genevieve and I were as alone in here earlier as we thought.

7

"Did you give them catnip or something?" Dad asks at dinner, staring at the cats as they run circles around the room.

He got to Grandma's house five minutes before expected and gave me a serious *Dad talk* after Sarah forced me to explain why I was basically in time-out. Even though I hated doing it, I lied and said that I *had* put the clothes in the sink.

Telling the truth would have made everything worse.

"We haven't given the cats any catnip," Genevieve says. "But they *have* been acting weird. They knocked over one of Grandma's vases."

"Huh," Dad replies. "That's strange. They're usually so careful."

He watches as the cats parkour around the room, leaping off furniture and chasing one another. I've never seen them so energetic.

"Yeah," Sarah replies. "Everyone's been acting a

little strange today." She looks at me when she says it. "Maybe it's a full moon."

I don't answer. I just eat my food and ignore her pointed remarks.

The sooner our stay here is over, the better.

×✗✗

After dinner, when the cats have finally tired themselves out and I've washed all the dishes—the final part of my punishment—Sarah grabs the keys.

"I'll be back," she says.

"Drive safe," Dad says.

She looks at me before she goes. "If I come back to find anything else of mine trashed . . ."

"You won't," I say.

"I won't let him out of my sight," Dad assures her. "Which, actually . . . how did he steal your clothes in the first place?"

Sarah hesitates.

"I was in the bathroom."

Dad flushes. "Ah."

Before it gets any more awkward, Sarah leaves.

Dad flops back on the sofa and turns on the TV to some local channel. Genevieve sits down next to him.

"Ew, Daddy," she says, wrinkling her nose. "You smell."

Dad grins widely and sniffs his armpits. "I do?" he asks. Then he grabs her and pretends to try to bury her head under his arms. Genevieve squeals and struggles away.

"Okay, you may have a point," Dad says. "I smell like the restaurant. I'll shower." He stands and points to Genevieve, adopting a mock-serious face. "I leave your brother in your wise hands, Genevieve. Don't let him get into trouble."

Genevieve is entirely serious when she replies, "I won't, Daddy."

Dad chuckles and heads into the bathroom.

I'm *so* glad they're having fun at my expense.

The moment we hear the shower run, Genevieve pulls me into the kitchen.

"What are you doing?" I ask.

"Shh," she replies. She drops her voice and looks around. When she looks at me, her eyes are serious and scared. "Did you do it?"

We haven't had a chance to talk since Sarah got home and accused me of ruining her clothes. It's clear Genevieve has been wanting to ask all night.

"What? No. Of course I didn't. I was by your side the whole time, remember?"

She bites her lip.

"That's what I was afraid of."

Someday she'll be old enough to match the way she talks. Someday.

She continues and asks, "But if neither of us did it, who did?"

I try to think of something witty, but I've got nothing. I just shrug.

Genevieve takes a deep, steadying breath, then looks me right in the eyes when she says, "I think the clown did it."

I can't help it. I laugh. Just a little.

Then I realize she isn't joking, and the laugh dies.

"You're serious?" I ask.

She nods. "Think about it. The cats have been acting strange ever since we went in there. I think they were trying to warn us."

"They're cats, Genevieve. They aren't that smart. They lick their own butts."

"That's for cleanliness," Genevieve retorts. "And I know you don't have a better explanation."

I want to give her another explanation. I even start saying, "I . . ." But then I stop. I've got nothing. She's right.

"We need to put the clown back," she says.

"But we're so close! And after what Sarah did to me—"

"That's more reason to put it back! You don't want

Sarah getting any angrier. You're already in trouble, and Dad won't find it funny if you're caught stealing from Grandma's bedroom."

Her fists are balled . . . and she can be stubborn when she sets her mind to it (just like the rest of us).

I know she's right. I don't need to be grounded all week. Again. Especially when I only did one of the things I'll be blamed for.

"Okay," I relent. "Let's go put the clown doll back while Dad's still in the shower."

She nods and we tiptoe down the hall to the guest room.

"I'll be lookout," she says, waiting at the door and looking toward the bathroom.

I roll my eyes and hurry over to the bed.

I pull back the cover and stop in my tracks.

"What's taking you so long?" Genevieve asks.

I don't answer. I can't.

This doesn't make any sense.

Genevieve tiptoes over.

"Don't tell me you're—"

She pauses.

"Please tell me you did this," she whispers.

I shake my head.

I'd been in the bedroom for most of the day. I only

left for dinner, and I know that no one else came in here.

And yet.

The doll . . .

It's gone.

8

There isn't much time.

We tear through the room, pulling back all the covers and looking under the bed and cots for the missing clown doll, hoping against hope that—I dunno—the cats grabbed it and tossed it somewhere. Somehow.

It isn't anywhere.

"I know it was here. I *know* it," I whisper. "I checked when I was grounded."

When we hear Dad turn off the water in the shower, we give up.

"Maybe it was Sarah," Genevieve suggests as we remake all the beds—we don't want to leave a trace.

"Why would she do that?"

"To frame you? To freak you out? I don't know."

"Maybe."

It's the only possible, plausible explanation.

Either that, or the clown doll walked out on its own.

Which is impossible.

Right?

If the clown got out, my stupid traitor of a brain asks, *where is it hiding now?*

I don't have an answer to that, and I don't want one.

It has to have been Sarah. I bet when she came in and saw the doll, she decided to turn it against me. I bet *she* shoved the clothes in the sink somehow and then hid the doll somewhere else.

Just to mess with me.

To put me on edge.

Though I would have figured she'd have hidden it in my bed to send a message.

Maybe she put it back in Grandma's bedroom?

I don't get the chance to look—Dad steps out of the bathroom in his pajamas, and he'll definitely notice us sneaking into Grandma's room.

All we can do is wait and wonder what Sarah has in store.

XXX

By the time Sarah returns home, I'm convinced she planned all of this to get back at me for trying to scare her in the first place.

Well, she's not going to scare me. I'm onto her.

We spend the rest of the night watching an old movie in the living room.

The cats continue their strange zoomies the entire time. They chase after one another and skid across the kitchen floors, then tackle one another and roll across the carpets.

"Let's hope they tire themselves out soon," Dad says, "or it's going to be a long night."

I'm not focusing on the cats, however. I'm watching Sarah, looking for any sort of tell that she had something to do with the doll's disappearance. But she's just watching the movie and texting her friends like absolutely nothing is strange.

Her calmness only puts me more on edge.

xXx

Thankfully, the cats settle down halfway through the movie, and for a little while I can forget about how strange the night as been. But just as the movie ends and we are about to head to bed, something crashes in the kitchen.

Dad jumps to his feet, exclaiming loudly about the cats, and runs in.

Sarah and I follow in his footsteps.

The kitchen is a disaster.

Somehow, the cats have knocked all the plates I left drying by the sink onto the floor.

Dad is already grabbing a broom, muttering under his breath as he cleans up the mess.

"Man," Sarah says. "What has gotten *into* them?"

First the vase, and then the plates? I'm positive the cats have never done anything wrong in their lives.

As I turn to go back to the living room, a dark shadow darts from the doorway and down the hall.

Tibbits, I think.

Genevieve is standing by the sofa when I get back to the living room. She's biting her lip and looking around anxiously. When I step in, she rushes over.

"What's up, twerp?" I ask.

"The cats," she whispers.

"Yeah. They're on a rampage tonight."

"No," she says. She looks around again, her eyes wide, before pulling me down close so she can whisper in my ear. "The cats were here *the whole time*."

"What are you talking about?"

"I saw them. They were under the sofa, right beside me."

"That's . . ."

"All three of them were there when the plates crashed."

She pulls me over and points under the sofa.

"They haven't moved," she tells me.

I get down on my knees and look. Sure enough, all three cats are huddled there. But I can see they aren't sleeping—their eyes are wide, and they look around as anxiously as Genevieve. My skin prickles with goose bumps.

"Are you sure?" I ask.

Genevieve nods.

"Something has scared them," she says.

She looks at me knowingly.

The clown doll.

I think of the shadow I saw dashing off down the hall, and the goose bumps multiply. Someone or some-*thing* has been causing mischief in the house. And if it's the clown . . .

I tell myself it doesn't matter. Tomorrow morning we'll be out of here and back in the safety of our house. Away from the creepy dolls that are toying with my imagination. Back to reality.

I just can't lose my cool before then.

9

I can't sleep.

Partly because Sarah is snoring and partly because, every time I close my eyes, I hear scurrying in the hallway.

I know it's just the cats. Obviously it's just the cats. It's night, they're nocturnal creatures, and every time I've ever stayed over here, I've been kept up by their antics.

This time, though, it sounds . . . different.

The footsteps sound heavier.

And it sounds like there are more than three sets of them.

Get ahold of yourself, I think. There's no such thing as possessed dolls. The only thing I need to worry about is Sarah and whatever devious plan she's hatching to get back at my attempted scare.

I roll over on the cot, trying not to make any noise because Genevieve is a light sleeper. Although right now I'm the one awake.

Squeezing my eyes shut, I try to ignore how late it is and how tired I'll be in the morning. That never seems to help me fall asleep.

I can just about feel myself starting to drift when another scurry of cat feet wakes me partway up. My head swims with that almost-asleep sensation, so it takes me a moment to realize a cat has come into the room. Which is strange, because they normally avoid the guest room and stick to the hall.

Whatever. Just so long as Tibbits doesn't hack up a hair ball on my face . . .

"Victor."

The voice is so soft I barely hear it. Coming from behind me, from under Sarah's bed.

It's also not a voice I've ever heard before.

My eyes snap open. I slowly turn my head to look behind me.

The bed is higher than the cot, so I have a front-row seat to the darkness beneath it.

For a few seconds, I look into the shadows and see absolutely nothing.

It's just a bed, I tell myself. *Just some darkness. Just the cats . . .*

"Victor," the voice whispers again.

It's high-pitched

        and childlike,

                and accompanied

by a frightening giggle.

Wake up, I think to myself. *This isn't real. You're just dreaming. This isn't—*

             Two

             red

             eyes

             blink

             open

             under

             the

             bed.

             Inch

             by

             inch,

             they

             start

             creeping

             closer.

"*Let's play, Victor,*" comes the voice. "*Hide or seek. You hide, and I'll come find you. Anywhere.*"

The red eyes lunge forward so fast I jerk back and nearly tumble off the cot. The whole thing squeaks as I cover my head with my hands.

Nothing hits.

Nothing attacks me.

"Victor?"

I look over to see Genevieve staring wide-eyed at me from her cot.

"What's going on?" she whispers. Sarah, somehow, is still snoring happily away in the bed.

"Nothing," I whisper back. I look around. There's no sight of anything in the bedroom. It has to have been my imagination. "I was just having a bad dream."

"No," she says. "You weren't. I heard it too. It was the clown doll you stole. It was coming for you."

10

I don't sleep at all during the night, not after the strange not-nightmare. I'm the first out of bed and spend the morning blearily watching TV and trying to stay awake. By the time Mom and Grandma get back in the early afternoon, I'm ready for a nap. Preferably as far away from here as possible.

"How did it go?" Mom asks.

"The cats were a bit funny," Dad reports. "Broke a few dishes. Sorry, Grandma."

Grandma looks at him with a funny expression, then glances at Sarah and Genevieve and me. I swear she's studying our faces.

I swear she knows we've been in her room.

I busy myself by texting Gareth and hoping Grandma can't read my mind.

"Is that so?" Grandma asks. "Well, I suppose it has been a while since they've been here without me."

"I bet they missed you!" Genevieve says, all cutesy.

As if she's not also terrified of clown dolls running around Grandma's house.

Or maybe, like me, she finds that harder to believe in the light of day. We were probably just overtired. Daydreaming. Whatever.

"Well, not as much as I'll miss you three! Come give your grandma a hug."

One by one, we go in for a hug with Grandma. I'm last.

She hugs me tight, for a few seconds longer than the others.

Right before she lets me go, she whispers into my ear, "Did you go into my room?"

I freeze. "What? No," I whisper back.

She gives me a squeeze, then smiles as if she didn't just whisper anything.

Does she know? *How* would she know? Unless she has the location of every creepy clown doll in there memorized . . .

"Got everything?" Mom asks. We all nod, then Genevieve and I pile into Dad's car while Mom and Sarah drive in hers.

Genevieve and I sit in the back seat.

"I think she knows," Genevieve whispers to me.

"What are you talking about?" I ask.

"That you took the doll."

"I didn't—" I lower my voice and glance at Dad. He isn't paying attention to us, or at least, he's pretending he isn't. "I didn't take anything. We moved it from one room to the other. It's still there. So I didn't take anything."

"Yeah, right," Genevieve replies.

I don't argue with her, though. There's no point. Mostly because she always wins.

So I make plans with Gareth to do a few more dungeon crawls tonight and tune out the rest of the drive home. I gotta finish my homework so he and I can hang out tomorrow.

We're the first ones to get home—I think Mom mentioned stopping at the store for something—and I head straight to my room to drop off my things.

Dad calls out that I need to clean up my room, and I roll my eyes, but he has a point.

Like usual, my room is littered with clothes and papers and books, and my bed is unmade.

Actually, wait.

No.

My bed *is* made.

I freeze in the doorway.

I know I didn't make my bed before we left. I know

because Mom gave me flak for it in the car ride over. Did . . . did Dad make it? But no, he went straight to Grandma's after work. So how . . . ?

That's when I realize that, although the sheets are pulled tight, there's something *else* in the middle of the bed, right below the pillow. A lump that shouldn't be there.

Every single nerve in my body starts to fire. Telling me to start walking backward and not stop. To run until I reach the next state and keep going.

I don't.

I don't know why, but instead my feet start leading me forward, led by my rational brain that says *there's nothing there but a pile of old clothes* while my irrational brain screams out that it will be much, much worse.

I reach out with a shaking hand.

My fingers touch the top sheet.

And I slowly

    peel

        the covers

           back.

        To find the same clown doll

          I'd hidden in Sarah's bed,

            now hiding in mine.

I can't help it: I yelp and stumble back, tripping over a pile of clothes and landing on my butt.

"What happened?"

I jerk my head over to see Genevieve standing in the doorway. She's looking at me like I've lost it.

"B-bed," I stammer. "C-clown!"

Her eyebrow rises.

"What are you talking about?"

"The clown! It's in my bed!"

"No, it isn't."

Her words are so calm, so assured, that I look away from her and toward the bed. I can't see anything from this angle, and slowly push myself to standing, ready to run from the room the moment I see that stupid red nose.

Instead, she's right.

"That's . . . that's impossible," I say. I rush over and yank back the sheets.

Nothing.

"It was right here!"

"Are you feeling okay?" she asks. She steps up beside me and peers under the bed. "There's nothing here besides stinky socks."

I collapse onto the bed and look at her. My heart is still hammering in my chest, but it's starting to slow. A little.

"I feel fine," I say as calmly and rationally as I can. "But when I got in, the clown doll was there.

Someone had made my bed and hidden the clown from Grandma's. And now, it's gone."

She sits down on the bed beside me.

"You have two options," she says. She holds up a finger. "One, there is a clown doll following you around and toying with you. Or two, you didn't sleep well and were hallucinating things. In science, the simplest answer is often the right one."

"I . . . You don't believe me? But what about last night?"

She shrugs. "I was sleepy, and we were in Grandma's creepy house, and you broke her rule."

I shake my head at her. The one person who might have believed me doesn't.

"You just need a good nap," she says. She pats me on the arm. "And to stop playing all those video games."

Then she heads out, leaving me feeling like I've just gotten a bad pep talk from Mom.

When she's gone, I look to the empty sheets and then hesitantly peer under the bed. I creep over to my closet and yank it open. I even kick a few piles of clothes to the side.

The clown isn't there.

"Maybe she's right," I mutter. "The simplest answer is probably the correct one, and the simple answer is that I'm just tired. But I'm not quitting video games."

The afternoon is a fairly normal blur. I do some homework and play some video games, Dad heads out to the restaurant to work, Mom runs errands, Sarah goes to practice with Alex, and Genevieve reads something way above her age level. A normal Saturday.

I don't see the clown again. Not even a hint of it. Which makes me begrudgingly think that Genevieve was right—I was probably just tired and riled up and seeing things that weren't there.

×✗✗

By evening, I've pretty much convinced myself that it was nothing. I don't have an overactive imagination or anything, so it's hard for me to continue to believe there's a possessed clown doll running around. The simplest answer is the best answer. I was tired. I imagined things. Case closed.

I'm lounging on the beanbag chair, dungeon crawling with Gareth on the other end of my headset.

"Over there!" Gareth yells out.

I flip my character around and blast a horde of zombies that had been creeping up on us from behind.

"Thanks, man," I reply. We keep going deeper into the dungeon. "I don't know what's going on with me. Staying at Grandma's really threw me off."

"I can tell," Gareth replies. He casts a lightning storm over another group of zombies farther off. "You're losing your edge."

"Dude, you don't even know. Earlier today, I thought I was being haunted by a clown doll."

"Hah! Seriously?"

"Seriously."

Gareth cackles. Even though he loves fantasy games like this, he's even more rational than me.

"Sounds like you shouldn't be playing so many video games," he says.

"Shut up. That's exactly what Genevieve said."

"It's melting your braaaaain," he taunts.

I roll my eyes and am about to blast another zombie when I see it.

A shadow along the wall.

I can't really see much through the glare of the screen, but I know something's different.

"Hold up," I say.

"What? We can't just pause here—" he begins, but I've already taken off my headphones.

The room is quiet.

Heck, the whole *house* is quiet. I know it's not too late—surely *someone* should be up right now—but I don't hear anyone else moving around in the house. No music from Sarah's room, no TV from the living room. Nothing.

It makes me feel alone.

I grab for my phone and, before I can scare myself, turn on the flashlight and point it at the wall.

Leaning against the wall atop a pile of clothes is

a

tiny

ceramic

clown

figurine.

Maybe the size of my hand. It holds a red balloon in one hand, and a dog sits hungrily at its feet.

My heart hammers in my chest. But I don't cry out. If Sarah's listening in, I'm not giving her that satisfaction.

"Nice try, Sarah," I say, hoping my voice doesn't shake too much.

I pick up my headphones and put them back on.

"What was that all about?" Gareth asks.

"Sarah," I reply. "She hid a stupid clown figurine in my room."

"I thought she hated clowns."

"She does. But I tried scaring her at Grandma's, and I think she's trying to pay me back." A little louder, I say, "It's not working!"

Gareth laughs and we resume the game. I slowly stop wondering how the figurine got there in the first place—I don't remember it being there when I sat down. But maybe I missed it? Who knows? I wasn't exactly scouring my room before starting the game.

It also makes me wonder where Sarah got the figurine. Did she steal it from Grandma's? I can't imagine she'd be that bold . . . but then again, I can't imagine her buying one from a store.

Eventually, the game consumes my attention, and soon I've forgotten all about the clown figurine.

Gareth and I level up a couple times, and eventually he says he needs to call it a night.

I yawn and agree, and we exit the game, promising to meet up in person to do homework tomorrow.

The moment I turn off the game and pull off my headphones, I remember the clown. It's the heavy silence that does it, that sensation of being completely alone in the entire world but also being watched.

I grab my phone immediately and turn on the flashlight.

When I shine it toward the pile of clothes where I last saw the figurine, my blood runs cold.

The clown is gone.

12

I turn on every light in my room after that.

For the next ten minutes, I search the room.

I poke through the piles of dirty clothes.

I pull back every sheet on my bed.

I root through my closet, pull out the books on my bookshelf.

I even poke underneath my bed with a base-ball bat.

Nothing.

There's nothing.

Not a single trace of a clown.

Finally, when I've gone over literally every square inch of the room, I give up.

"It's all in your head," I tell myself, looking around at the fresh mess I've created. I'm not looking forward to picking it all up tomorrow, and there's no way I'm doing it tonight.

When I'm sure the room is clown free, I curl up under the covers.

I may or may not hide my head under the sheets.

And I most definitely don't turn out the light.

Just in case.

13

"How'd you sleep, twerp?" I ask Genevieve the next morning.

She's already at the breakfast table, halfway through her cereal with a book open beside her. Knowing her, she's probably been up for the last couple hours.

Meanwhile, I feel like I've been hit by a garbage truck filled with diapers.

"Fine," she says. She looks up from her cereal and raises an eyebrow. "You look like you didn't."

I glance around the room. Mom and Dad are in the kitchen, and Sarah is still sleeping. I sit close to Genevieve and drop my voice to a whisper.

"Did you, um . . . did you see anything last night?"

To her credit, she doesn't laugh or raise her voice.

She whispers back, "What do you mean?"

"There was a clown."

"The doll?"

"No. A different one. One of those stupid little ceramic figurines."

"Where is it?"

I hesitate. "I don't know. When I turned the light on, it was gone."

She gives me a look. A look that very clearly says *I'm four years younger than you and even I can see that you're being ridiculous.*

"That's not possible," she says. "You must have been hallucinating."

"I . . . yeah. Probably. Unless, do you think Sarah—"

"Think I'm what?" Sarah asks, stepping into the room.

"Is ever going to get out of bed," I quickly cover. "Or if we're going to have to cover your chores."

"Riiight," she says. "You're whispering about *chores*. I know when you two are plotting something."

We aren't the ones who are plotting. At least, not anymore.

Genevieve and I stay silent, studying her closely. Will she admit it? Will she slip up?

Our silence only makes Sarah laugh.

"Well, whatever it is, it better be good," she says. "Because you know my motto."

"I don't get mad, I get even," intones Genevieve. "We know."

Sarah winks and heads into the kitchen to get breakfast.

"It had to be her," I whisper. "She practically admitted it just now. She's getting even!"

"The problem is, there's no way she would go anywhere near a clown, even if she wanted revenge," Genevieve says. She reaches over and taps my temple. "I think it's all in your head."

"You're probably right," I admit.

Not that it makes me feel any better.

14

Gareth comes over later in the afternoon.

I spent the whole morning cleaning my room and fully expecting to see a clown peering up at me from a clothes pile at some point, but nothing like that happened.

"So, clowns, huh?" Gareth asks.

I'm on the floor by my bed, notebooks and textbooks spread out around me, while he has his stuff spread out on my bed. I glance under the bed when he says it. All I find are shadows and wadded-up clothes I didn't want to put away.

"Yup," I reply. "Stupid, huh?"

He shrugs. "I dunno. Clowns are creepy. Those painted smiles? No, thanks."

"You're scared of clowns?" That's a new one.

"I wouldn't say 'scared.' More just . . . cautious. I don't trust them. Like, who in their right mind decides one day, *You know what? I'm gonna be a professional clown and scare children.* Can't be trusted."

I chuckle. I've known Gareth basically my whole life, but I didn't know he was afraid of clowns. Because I know him well enough to know that when he gets all explain-y like that, it means he's trying to rationalize something away.

Gareth is tall and Filipino, with choppy black hair that's currently dyed light blue and the bad habit of saying what he really thinks—usually in the worst situation possible. This means he gets in a lot of trouble in school and around the popular kids. That said, he's also the smartest kid in our class, so the teachers let his comments slide, and he does jujitsu, so the popular kids leave him alone.

Usually.

"Tell that to my grandma," I say. "Her bedroom was *full* of them."

"Really? That's strange—even for her."

He's been over to her house once or twice, so he knows what her house is like.

"I know."

"And now you think they're, what? Following you?"

"No, that's stupid," I say. "I think Sarah stole a few and is hiding them around the house."

I just have to ignore the part about them appearing and disappearing when she isn't around.

"Riiiight. Well, if you get too scared, you can stay over at my place. Possessed-clown-free zone."

"Thanks," I reply.

We work on homework for the rest of the after-noon, and then play video games until dark. It all feels so normal that by the time Gareth packs up to leave for the night, I've completely forgotten about the clowns.

"See you tomorrow," he says at the building's front door. "And keep an eye out for those creepy clowns."

So much for that.

I roll my eyes. "Thanks for reminding me."

He laughs and then heads toward his house. He only lives a few blocks away, so he's over all the time. I watch him go until he's around the corner. For some reason, I really don't want to go back inside. Even though everyone is home, I know what going back inside means—in a few hours, it will be time for bed. Time to close my eyes.

Sleep just makes me feel defenseless. Again, I don't think the clowns are after me. It's more that I don't trust Sarah not to sneak in during the middle of the night. Maybe I should get a lock for my door . . .

Before I can convince myself to go find a hardware store, I turn back into the complex and head up the stairwell.

When I round the corner at the second floor, I stop.

There, halfway up the staircase, another clown doll sits on the gross floral carpet.

This one is entirely made of fabric, one of those old-fashioned rag dolls with red twine for hair and big white button eyes. Its suit is blue and covered in felt stars, and its gloves and shoes are as red as its nose.

Red, like blood.

Red, like the smile painted on its face.

Its hands are folded neatly in its lap, and its legs are crossed.

As if it was waiting for me.

The moment I look at it, its head tilts to the side. As if watching me. Considering me.

My heart stops, just for a moment.

Then I convince myself it was just gravity, and let out a growl.

"*Sarah.*" A little louder, I call out, "Nice try!"

I try not to consider how Sarah managed to sneak up and down the stairs without me hearing. I step past the clown and walk—not run, *walk*—up the rest of the stairs to our condo. A part of me considers kicking the clown down the stairs, but I don't want to touch it. And if it was Grandma's, I don't want to get in trouble for damaging it.

Actually, on that thought, maybe I should bring it inside. Who knows if someone might steal it before Sarah can pick it up again? Then we'd all be in big trouble.

I turn back around to go grab it . . .

  . . . but the clown is already gone.

15

I *do* run up the stairs this time.

I run all the way up to our unit, and when I get back inside, I lock the door behind me. All the locks.

"Everything okay, champ?" Dad asks from the living room.

"Yup. Fine," I lie.

Before he can ask any more questions, I head back into my room.

All I can do is pace back and forth, my mind racing.

It couldn't have been Sarah. It just couldn't.

I had only gone up five steps before turning around, and that stairwell is *loud*. I can hear a Chihuahua coming downstairs from three stories up. There's no way a human—either a child or an adult— could have taken the clown without me hearing. There's nowhere to hide, and I would have heard a door open if someone was coming out of their condo.

Had it fallen?

But no, it wasn't at the bottom of the steps, and it's not like it would have rolled around the corner to disappear down the next flight.

There is only one answer. One simple, yet impossible, answer:

The clown doll had moved

all

by

itself.

It had gotten up and walked down the stairs while I wasn't looking. It's the only way. I would have heard any other footsteps, but I wouldn't have heard something as light as a stuffed doll.

But how?

Why?

Was it a smart doll? Some sort of new animatronic device created to freak out kids?

No, that makes even less sense.

A lot less sense than Gareth's silly warning: possessed clown dolls.

Is that it? Am I being haunted?

The moment the thought crosses my mind, I stop my pacing. It feels like this heavy weight just settles on my shoulders.

Because if I'm being haunted, I have no idea what to do.

A circle of salt? Light some incense? I'm not about to search the internet for what to do because I don't trust anything I read there.

You have to tell Grandma.

It's too late to call her, though. So I'm going to have to survive the night.

Should I talk to Genevieve? Sarah?

No.

Neither of them has said they've seen anything. Sarah would laugh at me, and Genevieve . . . well, I don't want to get her involved. I don't want to be the reason she's at risk.

The clowns are after me. Only me.

The question is . . . what do they want?

16

After I've scoured every inch of my room to ensure it's clown free, I pile a bunch of books and clothes against my closed door before going to sleep.

It's not a lock, but it's the best I've got.

Even then, I sleep with the light on.

Even then, I barely sleep at all.

When I do fall asleep, it's a fitful torment filled with nightmares.

Nightmares of tiny clowns clawing at my face. Of hundreds of clown dolls spilling from my closet or scrambling from under my bed.

Nightmares of a man's booming chuckle.

Nightmares that make me wake up, thrashing against my blankets and positive I've met my end.

Finally, shortly before dawn, I fall asleep and stay asleep.

When I wake up, it's daylight.

And I'm not alone in my room.

I can feel it before I even see it. The sensation of

eyes on me. The feeling of being watched. That terrible tingle on the back of my neck that says I'm not alone.

My heart races and fresh sweat breaks over my skin as I peer over my covers.

There, on my dresser, is the clown I saw in the stairwell, along with the porcelain figurine I saw the night before.

They just sit there, staring at me, their blank eyes and painted smiles somehow malicious.

For a moment I just sit there too, waiting to wake up. Then I look over to the door: My clothes and books are all undisturbed, still resting against the closed door. There's no way anyone could have gotten in here and gotten back out and moved those back into place. No way Sarah could have done it in the middle of the night.

I also have no idea how the dolls would have gotten in.

That's when I feel it. A slight breeze.

I glance over, and see that my window is open just a crack.

I know I closed it last night.

Chills race down my spine.

Did the clown dolls climb up to my room?

Were they hanging out outside my window, watching me toss and turn, waiting for me to fall asleep?

For some reason, that thought turns my fear to anger.

Before I can stop myself, I leap out of bed and walk over to the dresser. I grab the dolls and try not to notice how warm they are, as if they are alive, as if they have a pulse. I try not to notice how they seem to squirm in my hands—but that has to be my imagination, it has to be.

I head over to the window and manage to yank it open.

I hold the dolls out the window, the ground five stories below.

"If you can climb, let's hope you can fly," I growl.

I toss them. Hard. Away from the apartment and into the street.

I don't watch them fall.

I slam the window shut and turn around, then lean against it, panting hard. I wait to hear cars honk or the slam as the dolls crash against a garbage can.

Silence.

When I finally turn and look outside, peering down at the street, I don't see a thing.

17

"So let me get this straight," Gareth asks at recess. We're standing near the edge of the playground, as far from other ears as possible. We're also right beside a hedge, and I keep staring at it, expecting to see glass eyes staring back out. "You think there are clown dolls chasing after you. Like, possessed by ghosts or something. Like, for real for real."

I nod. My head throbs from the lack of sleep and the stress. I made myself comb the street before catching the bus to school. I didn't see a single sign of the dolls.

But I felt their eyes on me as I searched.

"For real for real," I admit.

Gareth whistles. "You know, I was kidding when I suggested that yesterday. Like, a joke. You know, like the one I'm pretty certain you're pulling on me."

"It's not a joke," I say. "I wish it was. I really do. I . . . Flaming pterodactyl."

His eyes widen.

So, here's the thing: Gareth and I play a lot of practical jokes on each other. It's why we became friends. Sometimes, those jokes involve really elaborate stories. One time, he had convinced me that his younger sister had been selected to perform on some European song contest and had flown off to Norway. In truth, she'd just gone to summer camp in Pennsylvania.

Another time, I concocted an elaborate lie about how our third-grade teacher, Mr. Hawkins, was actually an alien. I even doctored some photos to give fake evidence of him entering a flying saucer and having three heads.

When the games got too far, however, we decided we needed a phrase to signal that it was over. That we were finally telling the truth. Otherwise, we realized we'd stop trusting each other entirely—which almost happened after I brought Gareth some green slime I got at the dollar store and said I found it in Mr. Hawkins's desk.

The phrase was something ridiculous: *flaming pterodactyl*.

When it really sinks in that I'm telling the truth, Gareth slinks down onto the ground.

"What are you going to do?" he asks.

It's how I know he believes me, and it loosens a knot between my shoulders I hadn't known was there until just now.

"I don't know," I say. "I threw them out the window. I'm hoping they got run over, but I didn't see them after."

"Maybe they were cleaned up by a street sweeper?"

"They weren't the only ones, though. Honestly, the only thing I can think of doing is talking to my grandma. If they were hidden in her room, maybe she knows how to stop them from showing up again."

"Or she'll think you've lost it," he suggests.

"Not helpful."

"You wouldn't believe it if you weren't experiencing it," he says. He bites his nail for a moment, considering. "So they're just, like, watching you, right?"

"Yeah."

"That's good."

"Why is that good?"

He throws up his hands as if it should be obvious. "They aren't attacking you, that's why. If they're just following you around, I dunno, maybe they're just lonely or something."

"You really think so?"

"No. Not really. But I was trying to make you feel better."

"Mission unsuccessful."

Before I can ask him what *he* thinks I should do— he's always had a brain for elaborate stories and loves reading horror books—the bell rings. Time for the next class.

"Do you want me to go with you to your grandma's tonight?" he asks as we make our way toward the building.

"No. Thanks, though."

We get closer to the front door, and that tingle on my neck intensifies.

I turn.

There, in the hedge, I see the calico print of a clown doll's costume.

I yank Gareth's arm, spinning him around to see.

But just like all the other times, the moment I look back—and have Gareth look with me—the clown is nowhere to be seen.

18

I'm on high alert for the rest of the afternoon. Every time I turn around I expect to see a clown doll perched on a shelf, or hiding under someone's desk, or tucked away in the back of my locker. But—save for that one instance at recess—I don't see another clown doll for the rest of the school day.

"You're jumpy," Genevieve says as we wait for the bus. "What's wrong?"

"I . . . nothing."

"You're worried about the clown dolls, aren't you?" she says.

I look at her.

"Why would you say that?"

"Because you were real worried about it this weekend, and now you don't want to talk about it. You do that when things are bothering you."

"You should be a detective when you get older," I say.

"Nah. I'll settle for president."

She says it so confidently, I can't help but grin.

"You didn't answer me, though," she pushes.

My grin slips.

"Fine. Yes. I've been seeing them everywhere." *So much for not getting her involved. She's too nosy for her own good!*

"And you're sure you're not hallucinating them?"

No, I think.

"Yes," I say.

"Have you spoken to Grandma?"

I shake my head. "I was going to bike over there tonight."

"I want to come."

"What? No way."

"Why? It's just Grandma's house. Besides, I like being around her, and I want to show her the flowers I painted in art."

I stare at her for a moment. I consider telling her no, but I know her too well—if I say that, she'll just throw a tantrum or find some sneaky way of joining. Like telling Mom and Dad that I promised to take her, or something like that.

It's easier to just say yes.

She takes way too much after me and Sarah.

"Fine," I say. "But I don't want you bringing up the clowns. If she asks, I was the only one who went into her bedroom. You had nothing to do with it."

"Why?"

"Because . . ." *Because I don't want you getting hurt*. "Because I don't want you getting in trouble." I tousle her hair. "You gotta keep up your reputation of being an angel."

She bats off my hand and rolls her eyes.

"Just because I'm nice and smart doesn't mean I'm an angel."

"Noted. Guess I need to keep an eye on you."

She just grins. "Guess so." She considers for a moment, watching down the street as the bus comes into view. "But we should go now. Mom will never let us be out after dark."

"Good point. I guess biking is out."

I text Mom to let her know we're stopping by Grandma's on the way home, then catch the next bus heading to Grandma's neighborhood.

Genevieve and I sit in the front, near the driver. Genevieve happily hums to herself, watching the world go by. I can't stop looking around.

Every flash of red and I think it's a clown nose.

Every movement in the bus and I think it's a doll scurrying about.

I love my grandma, but I've never been so ready to get over visiting her in my entire life.

Finally, the bus stops a few blocks from her house,

and Genevieve and I walk the rest of the way. I know it's just my imagination, but I swear it gets colder with every block, the sky a little bit darker. Even though it's a normal day, and even though cars and buses drive down the street, and people are out walking their dogs or playing catch, I feel alone. On display.

At least I don't see any more clowns.

We knock when we get to the front door.

A few moments pass. No answer.

Genevieve rings the doorbell.

A few *more* moments pass.

The feeling of being watched intensifies.

"Maybe she isn't here," I venture.

Something moves in a window upstairs.

"I think I saw her," Genevieve says.

I'm pretty certain that wasn't Grandma. Maybe one of her cats?

I already know we aren't that lucky.

It's the clowns.

"Should we knock again?" Genevieve asks.

She raises her fist to knock, but before she can, the door just . . . opens.

She and I look at each other. Then, before I can stop her, she leans in and calls out, "Grandma?"

No answer.

My heart hammers in my chest. Once more, I

wonder if Grandma's gone over to one of her friend's places. It's not like she never leaves the house. She's actually really social and active in the community. She could be out helping in the community garden, or volunteering at the library, or teaching dance at the community center, or a dozen other things.

I don't know how I know that isn't right, though. The thought just feels . . . wrong.

As does this entire situation.

"Stay here," I tell Genevieve. "And get out your phone. Just in case."

For once, she doesn't argue.

I push open the door a little wider—

and nearly jump out of my skin when one of her cats—Tibbits?—races out with a yowl.

Genevieve yelps and dodges out of the way as the cat darts past her and runs into the bushes surrounding Grandma's house.

"What is *that* all about?" Genevieve asks.

Grandma's cats never leave the house. They *hate* it outside. One summer, we accidentally left the front door open all day while we played in her backyard. When we came inside, the cats were all lounging on the floor in a patch of sunlight, right on the interior welcome rug. They hadn't put a paw outside.

"Should I go get him?" Genevieve asks.

I peer into the bushes. I can see a patch of calico huddled there. Tibbits isn't going anywhere else—he just wanted *out*.

"No. Stay here."

I call out a bit louder to Grandma as I step inside.

It's eerie indoors.

Despite the sun shining outside, the curtains are drawn, letting in only a little light. A single lamp glows in the corner, casting harsh shadows on the walls.

The puppets glare down at me from their perches, and the dolls in their displays watch my every step.

"Grandma?" I ask again.

No answer.

I should turn around. This is rude, just walking into someone's house. But I can feel it in every cell of my body—something is wrong. Something that tugs me forward. I can't leave now. That would only make things worse.

I head down her hallway. To her bedroom.

The door is ajar.

My heart hammers. Her door is never ajar. Never.

"Grandma?" I whisper. My voice squeaks.

Slowly,

    ever

        so

       slowly,

                   I creep to her door.

My hand shakes on the wood as I push it open.

My breath comes out in a gasp.

Grandma lies passed out on her bed, her chest fluttering and eyes closed.

And every

    single

    clown

    in her room

        is gone.

19

"Grandma!" I call out. I rush to her side, then yell, louder, "Genevieve, come quick!"

I don't even get the sentence out before she's there.

"I thought I told you to wait outside?" I manage, anger and fear messing up my thoughts—I should be grateful, not angry, that she was here so quickly.

"You were taking too long," Genevieve says. She quickly walks over and hovers the back of her hand over Grandma's lips, then presses her fingers to her forehead. "She's alive. But she seems sick. Where are all the clowns?"

"That's not important," I say. "Call Mom and Dad. I'm calling 911."

She immediately gets on the phone, and I dial for an ambulance. I barely hear what the person on the other end of the phone says, just as I barely know what I say in return.

I can't take my eyes off Grandma.

I've never seen her like this before. Her skin is

waxy and coated with a light sheen of sweat, her lips purple and thin. She's always been so strong, even with her cane or walker—years of being a dancer made her a fighter, the perfect blend of grace and strength no matter her age.

But right now, she doesn't just look old. She looks like she's been drained of life.

Almost like I'd imagine a vampire's victim to look.

Honestly, I glance at her neck, just to make sure. There's no bite mark, but stranger things have been happening.

It also keeps me from looking around at all the empty shelves.

I want to wonder where all the clown dolls went. I want to think that she threw them out.

But I know better.

I know the truth.

They've been released. By me.

And now, they're on the prowl.

Soon, the room is filled with paramedics and my parents—I'm so out of it I don't even know who arrives first. I just know that in no time at all, both Genevieve and I are rushed out of the house and Grandma is taken away in an ambulance with Mom at her side.

"I want to be with her," Genevieve persists.

"Not right now," Dad says. "She'll be okay, but the paramedics say she's very dehydrated and needs a lot of rest. You can visit her when she's feeling better."

I stare numbly out the window.

"Do they know what happened to her?" Genevieve asks.

"Not yet, sweetie," Dad says. "But they will soon, I'm sure."

"She was just at the doctor's," I say. "Why didn't they see this coming?"

Dad sighs. "I don't have any answers, Victor. But we will soon."

We don't say anything else for the rest of the ride.

When we're back home, I head straight to my room and start my game. I should do homework, but I can't concentrate.

It's only when Genevieve comes in a few minutes later that I realize I'm so out of it, I didn't even get past the start screen. I've just been staring at the edge of the TV, thinking.

"It's the clowns," she says matter-of-factly.

I pull down my headphones to look at her.

"What?"

"The clowns. They're the reason she's sick."

"What are you talking about?"

She sits down on the bed, looking at me like I'm an idiot. Granted, right now I feel like one.

"They're the only things that have changed," she says. "Grandma was healthy when we saw her. She had all her clowns. Now they're gone, and she's sick."

"That doesn't make any sense," I say, a little gruffer than I intend. "She probably just realized that it was weird having all those clowns around, and got tired after throwing them all out."

"You're just grumpy because you know I'm right," she says. She gets off the bed. "You're also not asking the right questions."

"What's the right questions?"

"Why are the dolls after you, all of a sudden, and what do you have to do to make them stop?"

"They're not after me."

She sighs. "You really *are* grumpy. And that makes you stupid. But fine, suit yourself. Don't come crying to me the next time you see one."

Without another word, she turns and leaves.

I slip my headphones back on and actually start the game. I turn up the volume. I want to drown out my thoughts, and Genevieve's suggestions. But no matter how many explosions are onscreen, I can't block out her words.

She's right.

I know she's right.

Somehow, the clowns and Grandma's health are connected, and somehow both are connected to me.

Which means Grandma's sickness is my fault.

My responsibility.

I turn the game up louder.

20

We don't have a family dinner that night.

At some point in the evening, Dad comes in and sets a plate of pizza beside me.

At a later point, I know Mom gets home.

I don't turn off the game. I don't do any homework. And no one tells me to.

Eventually, my eyes start to hurt, and I decide to call it a night. I'm so tired I could fall asleep in my beanbag chair.

I turn off the game and blink away the stars in the darkness.

The house is quiet.

It must be later than I thought. I'm surprised no one ever came in to tell me to turn off the game and go to bed.

I'm even more surprised that no one came in to tell me what was going on with Grandma. It makes me fear the worst.

I stand and stretch and turn to go brush my teeth. The room is dark. But it's bright enough to see my bed.

To see the three new shapes sitting on the edge.

My heart leaps into my throat.

I pull out my phone and shine the light.

Three clowns. Each is clothed in shiny striped satin, with white porcelain faces and frizzy hair. Their faces are hungry, and it's easy to see why. The one with blue stripes holds a fork. The one with green stripes holds a spoon.

The one in red stripes holds a steak knife, and its smile is wicked.

Each stares at where I'd been sitting. As if they were about to eat me.

How long have they been there?

How long have they been watching me?

I want to throw up.

Especially because, as I stare at them, their eyes start glowing red. They lift their utensils.

And then, they start to speak.

"I'm coming for you," they intone.

The voice is male and angry, a single speaker coming from three porcelain lips. The words ricochet through me, fill my bones with cold and dread. I nearly fall to the floor in fear. Instead, I clutch my controller to my chest and consider throwing it at them.

"I'm getting stronger, day by day," the terrible voice says. *"And soon, you will be mine."*

"Who—who are you? What do you want?"

The voice cackles.

It sounds like a laughing grim reaper.

"You will know soon enough."

The eyes on the clowns go dark, and the room fills with ringing silence.

All I hear is my breath. All I feel is the thrum of blood in my ears.

Whatever was here is now gone.

After a few more minutes, when it's clear I'm truly alone again, I grab the clowns and shove them in my garbage can, then wrap the can in a blanket and tie it with belts. I don't want them in my room but I also don't want to risk throwing them outside—I know they'll just manage to escape again. This feels like the only safe option.

When I finally go to the bathroom, I turn on every light in the hallway. I brush my teeth as fast as I can, my heart still racing.

They can talk. There's something animating them.
I'm being haunted after all.

It must be late and I must be exhausted, because

none of those thoughts are met with resistance. I know in my bones it's true.

Something is possessing the clown dolls. Something that is after me. I just have no idea who or how or why.

I head back to my room. I don't flip off the hall lights, even though I know my parents will say something about it in the morning.

Back in my room, I freeze.

The belts and blankets on the garbage can are ripped open.

The clowns are nowhere to be seen.

I don't think I'll be sleeping much tonight, after all.

21

"Any more creepy clown sightings last night?" Gareth asks at lunch the next day.

"Three," I reply. "They were on my bed. Watching me play video games."

"Sounds boring for them," Gareth replies. "Unless they like watching people lose."

"That wasn't all," I say. "They . . . talked."

That cuts his humor short. He stares at me, his face suddenly serious.

"What did they say?"

I tell him.

Just saying the words brings the nightmare back to life. The burning red eyes, the deep voice that rumbled through my veins. I'd never heard that voice before, but now that I have, I know it will never leave me.

For a while after, we just sit there in silence. There's not much else to say, and my brain isn't working well enough to think of anything. I didn't sleep at all last night. Like, at all. My head hurts and it feels like I'm walking through jelly and there's this thick, sick feeling at the back of my throat.

"Any news on your grandma?" he asks after a moment.

"None," I reply.

"I'm sorry," Gareth replies.

I look at him.

"Do you believe me?"

"About the clowns, or about your grandma?"

"Both."

"Well, you did use the magic words," he says. "And you look like a zombie. So, yes. I don't think you'd go this far and break a vow to pull a prank. I just, you know, don't want to believe you, because I don't want it to be real."

He studies me for a moment.

"What do you think they want?" he asks.

"To scare me to death?" I ask.

"There are easier ways of going about that," he replies. "Honestly, it sounds like they're toying with you."

"Well, I don't like this game."

He sighs. "What have you tried? To, like, get rid of them, I mean."

I remind him about throwing them out the window and wrapping them up in the trash can.

"That's it?" he asks when I'm done.

"They keep disappearing," I say. "Sometimes before I can catch them."

"Hmm. Definitely toying with you, then."

I poke at my lunch. I didn't have breakfast and know I should be starving, but I'm too tired to even want to eat, which just makes me feel worse.

"What do you think I should do?" I ask.

He doesn't answer right away. I can tell he's giving the question serious thought.

"Maybe you have to destroy them. Like, fully destroy them. If there's a spirit possessing them, maybe that will get rid of them." He shrugs. "It works in video games."

"It's worth a try."

I yawn.

He looks at me with real concern.

"You need to get some sleep, man. You look terrible."

"Thanks. I feel terrible too." I rub my eyes. "I just can't sleep. I always expect to see one of them."

"Maybe I should stay over," he suggests. "I can be your backup. Clowns don't scare me."

"That may change," I mutter.

22

Another clown is in my locker at the end of the day.

I nearly scream out when I open the door and see it sitting inside, staring out at me with a grin. This one is entirely made of glass, with bulbous eyes and a too-large smile.

It's also pointing straight at me.

"What do you want?" I whisper.

"Talking to yourself again?"

I slam my locker shut and turn to see Sarah.

"What are you doing here?" I ask. She's in high school.

"I got out early," she replies. "And I figured I'd pick you up after yesterday." Her usual grin slips into real concern. "How are you doing, anyway?"

"I'm fine," I reply. I look to my feet. I am acutely aware of the clown doll in my locker.

"Are you sure? I know you didn't sleep last night. I saw your light on."

I shrug.

Do I tell her?

"I was . . ." I look around. A lump forms in my throat. "You won't believe me," I say.

"Victor," she says, her voice dropping into that soothing tone she only pulls out on occasion. "I'm your big sister. I know we joke a lot, but I'm here for you, okay? You can tell me everything."

I must be tired. Or desperate. Or scared. Or all three. Because tears start to form in my eyes.

"It's . . . clowns," I whisper.

I look at her briefly and see her tense up.

"What?"

I take a deep breath and—as quick as possible— blurt out, "Grandma had a bunch of clown dolls in her bedroom, and I took one out to try to scare you, but it disappeared and now all the dolls are out of her room and are following me and I don't know why but I think they want to hurt me and that's why Grandma is sick and, well, there's one in my locker right now."

She doesn't say anything.

Seconds creep past and I'm worried she's about to call the school nurse or something.

"Here," I say. "Look."

I pull open my locker.

I watch her expression.

Her face doesn't twist into shock or fear. Instead,

she stares past my shoulder with a worried look that quickly turns to anger.

"That's a really bad joke," she says. "On second thought, you can take the bus home. I'm going to go find Genevieve."

"Sarah, wait! It isn't a joke. I didn't put it there!"

She's already walking down the hall. But she does look back, just once, to say, "There's nothing there, Victor."

I turn and look back to my locker.

She's right.

The clown is gone.

As is my hope of getting her to believe me.

I let out a huge frustrated sigh and open the locker fully so I can rest my forehead on the door.

That's when I see it.

The scratchy writing on the inside of my locker.

At the exact spot where the clown doll had been pointing.

SOON.

23

They follow me the entire way home. I'm too anxious to sit on a bus, so I walk the entire way alone.

A large clown marionette dangles from a street-light. A dozen ceramic clown figurines in a shop window turn their heads as I pass. The stuffed bear with clown makeup peers out from beneath the bushes.

I see them, but no one else does. That's the problem.

I'm starting to wonder if they're really there at all.

I get home to find Genevieve and Sarah already there. Genevieve is doing her homework at the table, and Sarah is on her phone. The moment Sarah sees me, she makes a noise of disgust and leaves for her bedroom.

"What did you do?" Genevieve asks the moment Sarah is gone.

"Why do you automatically assume it's my fault?"

She just raises an eyebrow.

"Fine," I admit. "I told her about the clowns. I had one trapped in my locker. But when I tried to show her, it was gone. She thinks I'm pulling a prank on her."

"Well, you *were*. That's what started this whole mess."

I glare at her. I hate that she's right.

I sigh and sit down next to her rather than trying to fight her logic. "Any word about Grandma?"

"She's better," Genevieve says. "But apparently in a really heavy sleep or something. The doctors don't know what's going on."

"I just wish I could talk to her," I say. "She has to know what to do."

Genevieve just nods.

There isn't much to say after that, so I go to grab some cereal from the cupboard. Gareth should be over before dinner, but I'm starving—no breakfast or lunch isn't a good combination, apparently.

I pull down a bowl and begin to fill it with cereal, staring at my phone in a daze.

Then I hear something clink against the ceramic bowl, and look over . . .

To see a tiny porcelain clown figurine in a checkered suit smiling up at me from the cereal.

I yelp, and before I can turn away or let fear get the better of me, I grab the figurine.

It is disturbingly hot in my hand.

"Genevieve!" I call out. "Look! I got one!"

She hurries in and peers over my shoulder. I open my hands to reveal the tiny figurine.

"You're sure it's not just a toy that comes in the cereal box?" she asks. "I hear they used to do that, you know."

"When's the last time your cereal came with a toy?" I bristle. "No, this is one of her figurines. I know it is."

She peers closer.

"It doesn't look too scary to me," she says.

"Yeah, well, that's because they aren't following you around," I say.

Before she can say anything else, that terrible voice from before booms through my ears: *"For now."*

The voice shocks me so much that I drop the figurine to the ground.

But it doesn't shatter like a delicate ceramic figurine should. No—it ricochets across the floor and disappears beneath the fridge.

I don't go after it.

"Did you . . . did you hear that?" I whisper.

"Hear what?"

"The voice," I reply.

Genevieve looks at me, concerned. "I didn't hear anything."

"I . . ." I look to the space beneath the fridge. "But you saw that, right? You saw the clown?"

"Of course I did," she replies. She looks at me closely. "Are you feeling okay?"

"I'm fine," I reply.

I leave the cereal on the counter. I'm not hungry anymore.

Before she can ask me again if I'm feeling okay, I leave. I don't bother trying to grab the figurine from under the fridge.

I know without doubt that it's already gone.

24

Dinner that night is super awkward.

Gareth is over under the pretense of working on a school project together, which is great, but also difficult because Dad keeps asking details about the project, and Gareth keeps making them up on the spot. Genevieve isn't saying anything because she's really bad at lying, and Sarah isn't speaking because she's still angry at me and thinks I'm trying to prank her. Which basically means Gareth is the only one talking all through dinner, and by the time we get back to my bedroom alive I apologize profusely.

"I am *so*, so sorry," I say. "If I had known he was going to ask so many questions . . ."

"Don't worry about it," Gareth says. He flops down on my beanbag and grabs a controller. "On the plus side, if we ever do a presentation on the hybridization of feed corn, we've got it in the bag."

"Sounds . . . thrilling," I reply. "I hope that day never comes."

"We can only hope," he says. "C'mon, let's play before my brain melts any further."

I nod and grab some pillows from my bed.

Hiding beneath them are seven small ceramic clowns, each a different color of the rainbow, but each of them with sharp teeth in their red grins.

I yell out and stumble back, knocking into Gareth.

"Whoa whoa whoa," he says. "What's going on?" Then he looks to where I'm pointing. His eyes go wide. "I take it you didn't hide those there?"

I shake my head.

He stares at them for a while. Then he gets out of the beanbag chair and walks over.

"Wait, what are you doing?" I ask.

He picks up the nearest doll—the purple one—and turns it about in his hands.

"You're sure these are from your grandma's?" he asks.

"Positive."

"Well, let's be rational. It could be Sarah."

"But—"

"No, just hear me out. She hates clowns. But she knows that *you know* she hates them. So she'd be the last person you ever suspected."

"You said you believed me."

"I do! I'm also trying to think logically. Just for the

sake of argument. You said when you went to your grandma's, these were all gone, right? Well, what if she went in and took everything, and that shocked your grandma so much she, like, passed out or something? Sarah can drive. It's possible."

"It's also possible that a burglar is doing this to get under my skin," I say. "Or that aliens are doing it as some sort of experiment. Anything is possible, but that doesn't mean it's real."

"Okay, but—"

The next instant, the dolls' eyes glow red, and that terrible voice calls out, *"He is next."*

The voice reverberates through my skull, ringing in my ears and causing me to drop to my knees. I clasp my head in my hands and wince against the searing pain.

"Yo, dude! What's wrong?" Gareth asks. He drops the doll to my bed and crouches next to me, putting his hand on my shoulder.

"Did you hear that?" I gasp.

"What? What are you talking about?"

"The voice," I say. "The voice said it was coming for you next. And the clowns' eyes all glowed red, and—"

"Calm down. I didn't see or hear anything. There were no glowing red eyes. And no voice either." He hesitates. Looks at me a lot more closely than he usually does. Then he asks me the same question everyone else has all day. "Are you feeling okay?"

I burst.

"No, I'm *not* feeling okay!" I say. "I haven't slept and clowns are stalking me and everyone seems to think I'm losing my mind! Nothing is okay!"

"Whoa, whoa, calm down," he says, and I hate how much being told to "calm down" makes me do anything but. "I'm not, like, accusing you or anything. It's just . . . you aren't looking so good."

I let out a deep breath.

"What do you mean?"

"I mean, you look like you might be getting sick."

"I feel fine," I say. I push off his comforting hand and stand up. The first place I look is my bed.

Sure enough, the clowns are gone.

I point.

"There. Believe me? That wasn't Sarah."

Gareth's eyes go wide. He glances to the closed bedroom door. It's been shut the entire time, and I was only on the floor for a few moments.

"But there's no one else in here," he whispers.

"Exactly," I say.

"We gotta find them."

My stomach churns. "Good luck," I reply.

He begins rummaging around my room, trying to find any hint of the clowns. I don't bother joining him; I know that he won't find anything. The clown dolls only let themselves be seen when they want to be seen.

Instead, I look to the small mirror hanging above my dresser.

I hate to admit it, but he's right. I look terrible. There are dark shadows under my eyes, and my skin looks a little, well, waxy.

The churn in my stomach turns to ice.

I'm starting to look exactly like Grandma. Is this what happened to her?

Something rustles outside my window.

I look out and see a shape silhouetted in the glass. Hanging from my windowsill, five stories above the ground.

A single clown. The one I had originally picked up from Grandma's room and hidden in Sarah's bed. The one wearing striped satin, with big eyes and a bigger smile.

Now, those eyes burn red.

"He is next," the clown warns. *"Then I will come for your family. And when they are all mine, I will come for you."*

Then I blink, and the clown is gone.

25

"I don't think it's safe for you to stay here," I say to Gareth.

He's just combed through my entire room, and as expected, he hasn't found a single clown. He flops down on the bed beside me. Video games are definitely out for the night.

"What are you talking about?" he asks.

I tell him what the clown outside my window said. The moment the words leave my lips, he leaps from the bed and rushes over to the window, yanking it open.

"You should have said something," he says when he closes it. "There's nothing there."

"You wouldn't have seen it if I did," I reply. I flop back on the bed and stare at the ceiling. "They're toying with me. But if you're next . . ."

Gareth has this certain expression he gets when he's being stubborn—his jaw goes tight and his eyebrows furrow a little bit. And that's what he's doing right now.

"If I'm *next*," he says, "then wouldn't it make sense to stay the night with a friend rather than going home—at night, alone—to sleep in an empty bedroom where anything can get me? I might not even make it there."

I know he says that last bit as a joke, but a large part of me wonders if it's true.

"It might be safer than here," I say. "Where there have been multiple known possessed clown doll sightings."

"Just means we know what we're dealing with," he says matter-of-factly. "But, look, why don't we sleep in shifts or something. You sleep for three hours, then me. That way we each get a few REM cycles and your parents don't kill me for keeping you up all night."

"I don't think I can sleep," I say.

"You look like you'll pass out at any moment."

I know I should tell him my fears—that I'm somehow being drained like Grandma was. I just don't want him worrying about me any more than he already is. I don't want him continually asking me if I'm okay. It's more exhausting than not sleeping.

Instead, I pretend to yawn.

"Maybe you're right," I say. "I'll sleep first. You play some games. Set an alarm and we can switch."

"Roger that," he says. He grins. "Don't worry, I'll make sure no clowns get you in the night."

That's not what I'm worried about, I think.

Even though it's way too early to go to bed, I change into pajamas and get under the covers. Gareth turns off the lights and loads the video game, headphones on. I curl up so I'm facing him and the TV.

I tell myself I'm going to watch him the entire time. I'm not going to fall asleep and leave him at risk.

I tell myself I'm going to stay up the entire night, just to be sure.

I fall asleep immediately.

26

I walk down Grandma's entryway, and I know I'm in a dream.

I know because every time I turn my head, the world sways and blurs a little, and objects rearrange as if they've forgotten where they were supposed to be in real life. And every time I turn my head, I see flashes of red from the clowns' eyes I can't quite make out, even though I know they watch me from the shadows. Their laughter and skittering footprints follow my every move.

My feet lead me toward the hall.

At the far end, Grandma's bedroom door is ajar, just like it was when I saw her, drained and immobile.

Only this time, a sickly red light drips from the door.

Red, like the clowns' eyes.

Red, like blood.

I don't want to go in there, but I don't have a

choice. My feet guide me while clown dolls chase and tease around my legs. I look down, but all I see are thick shadows and flashes of red eyes and white teeth.

"Closer," comes the ghost's terrible voice from inside the room. *"Come closer."*

I do, even though every nerve in my body screams to turn around and run back.

When I finally reach the door, my feet pause. Glue themselves to the ground. It's my arm that takes on a life of its own. I reach up and push the door open farther.

If I wasn't dreaming, I would scream.

Red light fills the room, glowing from the hundreds of clowns' eyes staring down from every shelf. These clowns aren't the cheerful figures from the waking world. Instead, their eyes are sharp and evil, their teeth razors, their smiles turned to scowls. They all stare straight at the bed.

But I am not staring at them.

Instead, my vision is stuck on the shadowed figure in front of me.

It looks like a frozen whirlwind of black ink, a TV screen flicker of clawed hands and gnarled feet. Deep within that shadowy mass is a silhouette. A man. I can just make out the outline. I can just make out the red of his eyes.

The spirit floats in the center of the room. Then it

flickers, and it is right in front of me, only inches away. I try to leap back.

I can't move.

"Soon," the spirit growls. *"Soon I will be free. Soon I will take what is mine."*

It reaches out its hand, its nails like daggers, and stretches toward my face. The moment it reaches the space within the doorframe, orange light shatters across the space. Like an invisible electric wall. A force field.

Or a spell.

"Soon, I will be free. But until then . . ."

It pulls back its hand and flickers once more, returns to its spot in the center of Grandma's bedroom, right above her bed.

I think that's it. I hope it's over.

Instead, the clown dolls in the room all turn their heads

      oh

      so

      slowly

          and look to me.

Their evil grins widen.

One by one, they leap from their perches, crowding on the floor. They skitter toward me, cackling and calling while the shadowed spirit laughs.

It's only then that I realize I can move.

I stumble back, try vainly to get away.

But the hall suddenly stretches on forever.

The clowns push through the magical barrier and race toward me. Tiny hands grasp my ankles. Tiny teeth bite into my shins.

I can only just let out a scream before the tide of clown dolls washes over me and pulls me down to darkness.

27

I know something's wrong the moment I wake up.

Gareth is curled up in my beanbag chair, a blanket tangled around him. The game is still on, paused mid-battle, and the controller is at his feet. But that's not what has my attention, even though his skin is waxy and he's muttering in his sleep as if scared.

He has reason to be.

Around him, circled like lions around an injured gazelle, are a dozen clowns.

Ceramic figurines and glass statues, satin dolls and even the clown teddy bear. They are all staring at Gareth as he sleeps, some with hands outstretched as if grabbing at him. Their smiles are twisted, their eyes set in concentration. Even in the sunlight, I swear I see their eyes glow.

I stumble out of bed and knock the clowns out of the way. Gareth doesn't stir as the figurines roll away on the carpet, or as I kick the teddy bear into a pile of clothes. He doesn't move at all.

His eyes are closed tight, and sweat beads his brow. He seems to be writhing against . . . something.

"Hey, wake up," I whisper. I have no clue what time it is, but it's before my alarm has gone off, so we haven't missed school or anything.

He doesn't wake. Instead, he groans again and rolls over, curling into an even tighter ball.

I grab his shoulder and give him a shake, repeating a bit louder, "C'mon, wake up."

He reminds me way too much of the way Grandma looked.

When I look around, the dolls are all gone.

Blearily, he opens his eyes.

"Wh-what?" he asks. His voice is coarse and scratchy, and he doesn't actually look at me when he opens his eyes.

I don't tell him he had been surrounded by dolls. I don't want to scare him when he looks this sick.

"You were having a nightmare," I say. "Are you feeling okay?"

I put my hand on his forehead. His skin is cold and clammy.

"I'm . . . no," he says. "So tired."

His eyes flutter closed.

"You were supposed to wake me up," I say, even as I

berate myself, *Well, you weren't supposed to fall asleep! You were supposed to watch him, to keep him safe!*

Because even though it was a dream, I still remember every moment of the nightmare. That terrible shadowy creature. The horde of clowns. Even if I hadn't awoken to see him surrounded by clowns, I would have no doubt that Gareth is suffering because of it.

"Didn't . . . mean to . . . ," he mutters. "Just . . . quick nap."

I can hear other people awake in the house. My alarm goes off.

"You really don't look so good," I say. "I'll go get my mom."

He doesn't respond, so I rush from the room and head to the kitchen. Sarah stops me along the way.

"What's the rush, jerk?" she asks. Clearly, she's still upset.

"Gareth. He's sick."

"It better not be contagious," she says, holding up her hands and stepping out of my way.

Only if you're targeted by the clowns, I think.

✗✗✗

Twenty minutes later, Gareth's dad is in the apartment and picking Gareth up like a rag doll from the floor of my bedroom.

"We'll take him to the doctor," his dad assures me. "But he probably just caught the flu or something. That's what happens when you stay up all night gaming. You need to sleep. It's good for you."

He looks at me pointedly, and I know there's no use telling him we didn't play games all night. He wouldn't believe the truth. I barely do.

I watch them go. Gareth's head is resting against his dad's chest. Despite all the movement, Gareth hasn't woken up since I forced him awake.

"Is he going to be all right?" Genevieve asks. I jump. I didn't hear her come up to me.

"I hope so," I reply.

"Is it the clowns?" Genevieve whispers.

"Yes." I look to her. "You haven't heard or seen anything, have you? Like, you aren't being targeted?"

She shakes her head. "I thought they were just coming after you?"

"So did I," I say.

But I was wrong.

28

It's hard to focus at school. Partly because—even though I slept—I'm so exhausted I feel like I'm sleep-walking, and partly because—when my brain *is* working—all I'm able to think about is Gareth.

One more person to feel guilty about. One more person to worry over.

I'd asked Mom before leaving how Grandma was doing, and all she said was *stable*. I know that means she isn't getting worse, which is good. But it also means she isn't getting any better.

It's still up to me to help her—help *them*—but I'm no closer to finding out *how*.

It doesn't help that everywhere I turn, there are clowns.

Another three ceramic clowns rest inside my locker when I get to school.

One small satin doll is hiding in my gym shoes.

Two porcelain figurines peer out at me from behind the lunch counter.

Dozens watch from my classroom windows.

I ignore them. So far, they haven't done anything to hurt me. But I know they are there. I know they are watching. The memory of them attacking in my dream still feels like reality—at any point in time, they could strike. And there will be nothing I can do to stop them.

Which means, by the time the day is over, I'm even more tired than I was this morning. I can barely keep my eyes open as I trudge from my locker—another clown had been sitting atop my books, smiling wickedly— to the front of the school to wait for Genevieve and our bus. The only consolation I have as I wait for her on the front steps is that I haven't heard the terrible spirit voice again.

Minutes pass.

I check my phone.

Our bus will be here any moment, and Genevieve still hasn't arrived.

Which is strange—she's usually early.

I'm about to turn around and get her when I see Mom's car pull up. Sarah's in the driver's seat.

"What are you doing here?" I ask as she rolls down the window.

"Picking you up," she says. She doesn't sound happy about it.

"Why?"

"Because I'm being nice," she replies. "And because Mom is making me. Get in."

I'm too tired to argue, even though a small part of me wants to turn around and walk to the bus. Just to make a point. Even though I don't really know what that point would be.

I get in.

"What's wrong?" I ask the moment I'm buckled up.

"Genevieve isn't feeling well," she replies. She looks at me, then pulls out of the parking spot. "She came home early."

My blood goes cold, and any animosity I had toward Sarah vanishes.

"What's wrong with her?" I ask.

"Just sick," she replies. "No fever or anything. But she's super tired. Mom thinks she's got whatever Gareth has. Which is why she wanted me to drive you home—didn't want you infecting anyone on the bus."

"You think I'm sick?"

She glances over at me and raises an eyebrow.

"You look like the walking dead," she replies. "Only they're more animated."

I chuckle.

Just like that, I know the whole episode about the

clown yesterday is forgotten. Or, at least, she's no longer mad at me.

The laughter is short-lived. Because as we drive, a heavy dread falls over me: Grandma and Gareth and Genevieve are all sick. The spirit said it wanted my family. Will Sarah be next? Mom? Dad?

I can't let anyone else get hurt. I need to stop this. Now.

For that, I need Sarah's help.

"I need to go to the hospital," I say.

"Are you feeling sick?" she asks, her voice suddenly panicky.

"No," I say. "Sorry. Not that. It's just . . . I need to see Grandma."

"Dude, the whole point of me bringing you home is to keep you from infecting anyone else. Other than your unlucky family members like *moi*."

"I'm not infectious. And if you're really that worried, I'll wear a mask. It's just . . . I'm really worried about her."

We pause at a stoplight, and she gives me a searching look.

"Why do I get the feeling that that's not the only reason?" she asks.

"Because it isn't," I admit. "But if I tell you the truth, you'll think I'm lying. Please, Sarah. I'm worried that if I don't talk to her, what happened to her will happen to Genevieve."

The light turns green, and she starts to go. I desperately try not to notice the clowns sitting atop the streetlight like crows. No one else seems to see them.

"This isn't another prank?" she asks after a while.

"No. I'm serious."

She sighs. "Okay. Just don't tell Mom and Dad. They'd kill me. And yes, you're wearing a mask."

29

I don't know what's more surprising: the fact that Sarah and I are able to get in to visit Grandma without any issues, or the fact that I don't see a single clown in the entire hospital. The absence is eerie. It should make me feel free, but instead, it honestly makes me feel like I'm being watched even closer.

I almost preferred it when I could see them staring at me.

That fear is pushed from my head the moment we are shown into Grandma's room.

She doesn't look like she did when I found her.

She looks worse. Much worse.

There are IVs in her arm and monitors beeping away beside her. Her skin almost looks translucent under the harsh lights.

"Hasn't woken up since she came in," the nurse says as he shows us in. "But you're welcome to sit with her for a while."

"Thank you," Sarah replies. I can't find the words to say anything.

Instead, I flop down on the plastic chair beside her and watch her sleep. I want to take her hand, but I'm terrified that if I touch her, she'll just wither away or deflate like a popped balloon. So I keep my hands clasped in my lap and try not to cry.

This is my fault. This is all my fault.

"Grandma," I whisper.

"She can't hear you," Sarah says.

"I don't care," I reply. I don't look away from Grandma's face. Did her eyelids flutter, or was that my imagination? "Grandma, can you hear me?"

"You heard the nurse, she hasn't—"

Grandma moans and rolls her head.

"Oh my gosh, she heard you," Sarah says. She hurries over and kneels at my side. "Grandma, can you hear me? It's me, Sarah."

Grandma's eyes flutter open.

"Sarah . . ." Grandma's eyes focus on me. Her attention snaps. "Victor!"

She tries to get up, but Sarah gently pushes her back down.

"You need to rest, Grandma. Don't get up."

"I must . . . keep him contained . . ." Her eyes flutter again, and she falls back against her pillows.

For a moment, I'm terrified she's already passed out again.

Or worse.

"Contain him?" Sarah asks. "Contain who?"

"Mordeth," Grandma whispers. Her eyes open, but she doesn't look to me or Sarah. She stares at the ceiling and starts to silently cry. "He's nearly free."

"What are you talking about?" Sarah asks. She looks from Grandma to me. "What is she talking about?"

I think I know.

I lean forward and take Grandma's hand. She looks to me then, and her eyes are filled with terrible despair.

"You have to help me, Grandma," I say. "He's after me. After all of us. How do I stop it?"

Sarah gives me a confused look. "What are you talking about? Who's after us?"

"The dolls." It's not me, but Grandma who says it. "The clown dolls . . . they . . . contain him."

Sarah's eyes go wide.

Thankfully, Grandma keeps talking. Whatever strength she has left, it's clear she's using it up now.

"They must be returned . . . Only then . . . will he be bound."

"Returned? Back to your room?"

Her eyes shut.

"Grandma," I press. "Grandma, what happens if I don't return them? What happens if Mordeth breaks free?"

She doesn't answer. Instead, she gives one long, terrible cry of pain.

Then she falls back into a heavy sleep.

30

We sit there in silence for a while, watching her heart monitor steadily beep, watching her chest rise and fall. At least she's alive.

For now.

If I don't manage to get the clowns back into her room, I don't know how much longer she'll have.

"What. Was that. All about?" Sarah asks me.

"You wouldn't believe me if I told you," I say. I start to stand, but she reaches up and grabs me.

"No. You don't get to do that. What was she talking about? Who or what is this Mordeth? And what does it have to do with clown dolls?"

I look at her. For the first time in a long time, there's an expression that says she is ready to believe me. She actually looks a little lost, and it feels strange that she's turning to me for clarity.

"When I mentioned the clown in my locker the other day," I say. "That wasn't a prank. It was real.

I've been followed by the clowns that Grandma had hidden in her bedroom."

"What? Why?"

I lower my eyes. "I wanted to scare you. When you went to band practice and left Genevieve and me alone. I was going to plant one of the clowns under your pillow. And I did! But then it ran off. I think that's what started it. Now all the clowns that were in Grandma's bedroom are gone, and it sounds like we have to put them back. Otherwise . . ." I look to Grandma. "Otherwise, what's happening to her will happen to Gareth. And Genevieve. And eventually all of us."

"This doesn't make any sense," Sarah protests. "This is real life—there aren't such things as evil spirits and haunted clown dolls or whatever."

"I want that to be true," I say. I look at her very seriously. "But it isn't. This is real. You heard Grandma. We have to put the dolls back."

Sarah opens her mouth to protest. Then she looks from me to Grandma.

"You really think this will happen to Genevieve?" Sarah whispers.

"Yeah. And Gareth. And everyone else in our family if we don't stop this."

She takes a deep breath. "I really wish this was all a bad joke."

"Me too."

She closes her eyes and nods. "Okay, then. How many are there?"

"Hundreds," I say.

"Of course there are," she says. "Just my luck."

31

Sarah and I devise a plan on the drive home. It's not much, but it's all we have, and honestly it's a miracle that she believes me.

It's also a miracle that she's willing to put herself at risk.

At first, I don't think it's going to work. Then, a block from home, she slams on the brakes.

"Is that . . . ," she begins. She points to the tree on the opposite corner.

To where a clown is hiding, watching her with a malicious grin.

"Yeah," I say. "He knows you're aware of them now. You're a target."

"Great," she says. "Just great."

She keeps driving. I notice her hands are tight on the wheel, and she doesn't blink. Not until we've parked.

We go through the evening as normally as we can. We both check on Genevieve every half hour. Our little sister is curled up in bed, and I swear she looks worse every time I see her. We have to work fast. For her sake and Gareth's.

We also have to work fast for Sarah. Because as the night wears on, it becomes clear she's seeing the clowns just as much as I am. She continually holds back gasps or screams when opening the cupboards or staring out the window. Even *she* starts to look tired from always being on alert, and she's only been aware of it for a few hours.

Either that, or the spirit—Mordeth—is getting much, much stronger.

"I nearly forgot," Sarah says after dinner. "I have band practice tonight."

"Just make sure you're home before ten," Mom says.

"Can I go?" I ask.

Mom raises an eyebrow.

"Please?" I press. "I've finished all my homework."

"But you might be contagious."

"If I am, so is she," I say. "We drove home together, after all."

Mom sighs heavily.

"He has a point," Sarah says. She does her best to sound grumpy and not like this was her idea all along.

"Not that I want the twerp around, but it might be good for us to practice in front of an audience before the show."

"Don't worry, I'll tell you if your music bites," I say.

"See what I mean?" Sarah says.

Mom considers. "Fine," she says finally. "But in that case, home by nine, got it? And you better have gotten all your homework done, mister. If I find out you were lying, you're grounded."

I nod, relieved and trying not to show it.

"Also," Mom says, "if *either* of you starts feeling sick, you come home immediately. I don't want you giving the rest of the band anything, and you aren't performing if you're ill."

"Got it, Mom," Sarah says. "I'm sure no one else will get sick."

Ten minutes later, after we've helped clean the dishes, Sarah and I are in the car and heading not toward Alex's for practice but to Grandma's.

"Are you sure this is going to work?" she asks. It's the first time she's sounded nervous during all this, which makes me nervous. But it's not nerves that it won't work.

I'm nervous that the first part of our plan will work too well.

"I'm pretty certain," I say. I nod out the window.

We're at another red light, and when Sarah looks over she sees what I'm staring at: half a dozen clowns dangling from the trees, hanging like monkeys in the park. Their red eyes glare at us.

"There are more of them than before," Sarah says. She shudders.

"They know you're afraid of them," I say. "And they like it."

She doesn't say anything to that. It's not a good feeling to know that your fear makes something . . . hungry.

We park outside Grandma's house.

Even though the sky is still a little light, it feels colder and darker here. The air feels . . . wrong. I start to get out of the car, but Sarah doesn't budge.

"What is it?" I ask.

"Look."

I look to where she's staring.

The clowns

       are

            e v e r y w h e r e.

They perch in the trees and hide behind the fire hydrant. Some peer from car or house windows. Others glare up from the gutters. Everywhere we turn there are clown dolls. Including the one that started the whole thing. It sits in front of Grandma's door, smiling at us placidly.

Welcoming us to our doom.

"If anything goes wrong in there," Sarah begins.

I cut her off. "Nothing will go wrong."

"But it might. And you have to listen to me because I'm your big sister. *If* anything goes wrong, you leave. You run home and *make* Mom believe you, and then you take Genevieve to the hospital and . . ."

She trails off. We both know that there's no alternative ending to this. We both know that if this fails, we're all doomed. No matter what.

The doctors can't save us. Our parents can't save us. No one can but us.

"Let's go," I say.

Sarah nods and tears her eyes away from the clowns. She grabs her guitar case from the back seat, and I sling on my backpack.

Together, we walk into Grandma's house.

The clowns' eyes follow us the entire way.

32

It feels far too much like my dream.

The lighting is harsh and tinged with red, and just like before, I feel my footsteps pulling me forward. This time, however, I'm able to resist them. Sarah and I both pause in the living room and look around. It's eerily silent—one of Grandma's friends took the cats to her house. So the cats aren't around . . . but we still don't feel alone.

The hundreds of dolls and artifacts Grandma collected over the years—the ones that don't have anything to do with clowns—glare down at us. Their eyes are accusing—it feels like they all know what we did, what *I* unleashed, and they're angry for it.

"What now?" Sarah asks.

"Now we act," I reply.

I know the clowns won't go into the bedroom. Not on their own.

"Are you ready?" I ask.

"No," she replies. "But let's do this anyway. For the record . . . clowns still really, really freak me out."

"I know," I say.

Before I can talk myself out of it, I turn around and go back to the front door. The clown is still there.

It isn't alone.

A good fifty clown dolls are arranged on Grandma's front steps. It looks like they've frozen mid-climb, their arms raised and faces trained on the door. A frightening photograph, but in real life.

I want to scream and slam the door in their terrifying faces.

Instead, I lean over and pick up the original clown doll. It nearly burns my skin, but I don't drop it. I bring it inside.

I don't close the door behind me.

"What are you doing with that?" Sarah asks loudly. She takes a step backward, and although this was all part of the plan, I still feel bad as I raise the doll up to her face. "Get it away from me."

"But it wants to play with you. Come on, don't tell me you're scared."

She takes another step back and stumbles against Grandma's coffee table, nearly tripping over it.

"Victor, stop it. Please. This isn't funny."

"Yes, it is," I say. "After all you've done to me, this is *hilarious*."

Her eyes go wide as she looks over my shoulder. I don't turn around. I don't need to. I can feel the clown dolls swarming into the room behind me.

I still don't know precisely what Mordeth wants, or how this all works, but it seems that he deals in fear. He's picked off my friend and family, used their fear to drain them. He's been slowly draining me as well, keeping me awake, forcing me to always wonder where and when another clown doll would appear.

If he wants fear, Sarah can give it to him. Like she said—clowns still really freak her out.

"Victor, please," she says. "Keep it away from me."

"Don't you want to play?" I ask.

"I'm done playing. I'm sorry for leaving you alone. I'm sorry for everything. Just, please, make this stop. Make them all go away. There are so many of them."

I turn then and look. She's right. There are hundreds of dolls in the room, jostling for space among the knickknacks and figurines. They pile up on the sofa, cram into the bookshelves.

I don't see any more of them outside.

"You're right," I say, turning back to her. It's time. "They're all here."

That's the cue. Immediately, I race back to the front door, slamming it shut and locking it tight. The moment I do, Sarah leaps into action and yanks open her instrument case, revealing dozens of garbage bags. She starts grabbing every doll she can find, stuffing them into the garbage. I'm right behind her. I yank out the plastic bags I'd hidden in my own backpack

Up until now, the dolls just appeared and disappeared. I never saw them move, save for turning their heads or smiling.

Now that's no longer the case.

They come alive.

And they don't want to be caught.

My skin crawls as the clown dolls swarm up the shelves like spiders or ants, scurrying over Grandma's priceless artifacts and knocking them to the ground. I leap out of the way as a large vase falls where I'd just been standing, then grab for a ceramic clown that tries to leap past me. It struggles in my hands as I shove it in the bag, thrashing against the plastic. I grab another that tries to race past my feet. My vision is a blur of scuttling clowns, my breath harsh in my chest as I race after them. My breathing is hard, and my lungs hurt like I'd run a mile in gym, and I know deep down it's not because I'm unused to this sort of cardio—it's because Mordeth has started to drain me too. My arms feel like I'm struggling through water. But I keep going.

My trash bags bulge as I shove in more fighting clowns. My arms are covered in scratches and tiny bite marks, and I hear Sarah grunting and yelping as the clowns fight her off. But she's tough. Tougher than me.

Which is why, when she yells out, my blood goes cold.

I look over to see her covered in clowns that scratch and kick at her. Her trash bag is forgotten at her side, and more clowns are spilling out . . .

I run over with my bag and start yanking clowns off of her. They kick and scream in my hands, but soon Sarah is up and helping as well. Being attacked seems to give her renewed strength—she throws the clowns in the bag with full force, yelling every time. I'm pretty certain she breaks half of them.

"Thanks," she huffs.

"No problem," I reply, grabbing a clown from the top shelf and throwing it in another bag.

Soon, the living room is filled with bulging bags, each of them squirming and writhing as the clowns within try to break free.

We prepped and triple-bagged, so that's not happening.

"Is that all of them?" Sarah asks. She's huffing and puffing, but she isn't nearly as winded as I am. I lean against the wall, barely able to stay upright.

I look around the room. It's easy to see every bit of space now that the clowns destroyed everything. It looks like a tornado swept through. Guilt twists in my stomach. As well as a small note of relief.

"I think that's all of them," I say.

"Okay, then," she replies. "Let's drag them into the bedroom and get this over with."

"No," I reply. "I started this. I think I have to be the one to end it."

"But—"

"You stay out here. Keep watch. Make sure we didn't miss any."

She opens her mouth to protest, then closes it. "You sound like the older sibling now."

I grin. "At least I don't look like it."

She sticks out her tongue.

Then, before I can change my mind, I grab some of the bags and begin hauling them into the bedroom.

I fully expect to feel something as I cross the threshold to Grandma's bedroom. A shiver of energy. A jolt of cold, or a wave of heat. But I don't feel anything.

I toss in the first few bags, then go back and grab the others. Sarah watches me silently, her arms wrapped around her chest like she's hugging herself or trying to hold herself back from helping.

In no time at all, I hold the final bag in my hands. It squirms under my grip.

"Here we go," I tell Sarah. "Last one."

"I just hope this works," she says.

"Me too," I reply.

I haul the last bag into the bedroom and toss it onto Grandma's bed.

Nothing happens.

I stand there, surrounded by all these bags of clowns, and I realize they're no longer moving or squirming.

The house is completely silent.

I did it. I think.

"Is it over?" I whisper. "Is that it?"

A beat passes. Still, I hear nothing.

I wait a few more moments. Fear is slowly replaced by relief.

Finally, I let out a huge sigh.

We did it. We put back the clown dolls. Everyone is going to be okay.

I turn to leave the room, and just as I do, I hear that terrible booming voice. Only it's not coming from the bags or the bedroom. It's coming from the living room. From where Sarah is.

"You didn't really think it would be that easy, did you?" growls the voice.

The next moment, the bedroom door slams shut and Sarah begins to scream.

33

"Sarah!" I call out, banging my fists on the door.

"Victor!" she yells back. "Help!"

But her yells aren't all I hear.

Behind me, the room erupts into maniacal cackles.

I turn in horror to see the clowns bursting from their bags. Their eyes glow red and their mouths are filled with sharpened teeth. I've trapped myself in here with them. Just as I've trapped Sarah in the house with Mordeth.

This whole thing has been a trap all along.

Just like in my dream, the clowns swarm after me, scuttling like ants and grabbing me with their tiny gloved hands.

I kick and shove, trying vainly to knock them away. But there are too many. I cry out in pain as they begin biting my legs, clawing at my skin. This is not how I want to go. I stumble backward, tripping over a clown and landing on my back. Instantly, they are on me. They bite and scratch and claw, and no matter how much I thrash about I can't get them all off me. They pile on top of me, pressing the breath from my lungs and covering my eyes, so all I see is darkness.

Darkness, and glowing red eyes.

The energy starts to leave me. I've lost. We've all lost. This is my fault, a prank gone wrong, and I deserve to be punished for it.

I feel myself letting go, feel my body shutting down.

The clowns have won.

Mordeth has gotten the last laugh.

As the darkness closes in, as Sarah's screams fade from hearing, I feel myself sinking, feel the weight of my bad decision pressing the life out of me.

And then, I hear her.

Genevieve.

Her voice is distant. Angelic. I must be hallucinating her, because she's at home, sick. Fading. Relying on me to save her, even though I've failed. Except rather than fading, her voice gets louder.

Yelling.

Calling out.

Then, light.

"Get! Away! From! My! Brother!" Genevieve yells.

More dolls are batted away to the side, and I can

see it now, can see my younger sister standing above me, a baseball bat in her hands.

It's her. It's really her.

She keeps hitting and kicking away the dolls, and now that some are off me, I'm able to thrash the rest of them off myself. I manage to push myself to standing, and she throws another baseball bat toward me. I grab it, and together we knock the rest of the dolls down. Some shatter. Some just skitter away. Others try to fight back.

Ceramic dolls leap at my face, and when I swing my bat, they explode in clouds of dust. Fabric dolls climb up Genevieve's legs, but she swings her bat like a golf club and sends them flying.

"What are you doing here?" I ask as I knock back a clown that leaped from atop the dresser.

"Saving your butt," she replies. She kicks another small clown doll away.

"I thought you were sick!" I say.

"That was a fakeout," she replies. She smashes another doll away. "After Gareth got sick, I figured they'd either come for me or Sarah next. And I knew that would make you try to find a way to solve things and end up needing my help. So I hid in my room and listened, and when you left, I snuck out."

"How did you get in?" I ask. I kick away a trio of

glass dolls that had been trying to climb up my leg. "The doors are locked."

"The window," she says, nodding to the bedroom window right before hitting a ceramic doll off the shelf. "You didn't lock this one. But I did, behind me."

We keep smashing away clowns as we speak, but no matter how many we knock down or break, more keep coming.

"We can't keep going like this," I say. "We have to get to Sarah."

"Is she in the living room?" Genevieve asks.

"Yeah. But the door is jammed or something."

"I bet we can get it together, but we have to hurry. I don't hear Sarah anymore."

We bash aside another wave of clowns, and then start working on the door. Together, we give it one big pull and manage to yank it open. We rush into the hall and slam the door shut behind us.

"Here," Genevieve says. She pulls a skeleton key out of her pocket and locks the door, then hands the key to me. "I took it from Grandma's purse. Just in case."

"You are full of surprises," I say.

She grins but goes serious immediately.

"Speaking of surprises," she says, and nods down the hall.

I look to see the original clown standing at the far end.

Life-size.

Almost human.

It smiles widely when it sees us and waves.

"You made it out," it says. *"Now we can really have some fun."*

34

The clown races forward, moving faster than should be possible.

It lunges toward us, and Genevieve and I duck out of the way just in time. Genevieve screams out as the clown swipes at her head, but she dodges and darts off toward the living room.

"Leave my sisters alone!" I yell out, swinging the bat at the back of its head with all my might.

The clown spins on the spot and catches the bat with one clawed hand. Its smile widens, its eyes the deepest glowing red.

"It's not your sisters I'm after," it says. *"It's you I want."*

Its fingers tighten on the bat and easily crush the part it's holding to dust. I drop the rest of the bat to the floor and run to the living room.

What I find is almost more terrifying than the clown itself.

Sarah is passed out on the sofa, her skin as pale as

Grandma's and her breath shallow. At least I don't see any more wounds. Instead, she looks drained to the point of death. Genevieve kneels at Sarah's side, tears in her eyes.

"She won't wake up," Genevieve sobs.

"Get her out of here," I reply. "Call an ambulance, but get her out of this house!"

Genevieve nods, and together we begin to lift Sarah from the sofa.

We don't get far.

"Now, now," the clown—Mordeth—says. *"Why would I let you go when I finally have the whole set?"*

It towers in the hallway, its head now brushing the ceiling. Its arms are bent and broken, its face contorted and filled with razorlike teeth.

"What do you want from us?" I yell out.

"Freedom," Mordeth growls. It takes a slow, menacing step closer. *"For generations, I have been contained within this doll, passed down through your family like a toy. Did you know? Did you know your grandmother—and her grandmother before her—was a witch? And that one of you would one day follow in her footsteps?"*

My eyes go wide. I look to Genevieve. She stares back at the clown with anger clear on her face.

"I was growing stronger," Mordeth continues.

"*And your grandmother knew it. She split my soul into a hundred pieces and bound them to various dolls. Then, she contained those dolls to her room. She weakened me, but she did not destroy me. All I needed was for someone to bring me past the barrier. All I needed was* you."

Mordeth's eyes burn into me, spearing me to the spot.

I was right. This *is* all my fault.

"*Once you brought one of the dolls out, the spell was broken, and I was free. But I still required energy. I required your fear. In haunting your relatives and friends, I could draw their life force into me. Your elder sister has nearly refilled my strength.*" Mordeth turns its deadly gaze to Genevieve. "*Now, I require the fear of only one more, and I will be unstoppable!*"

It leaps toward Genevieve like a spider monkey, knocking her to the floor and ensnaring her there. Its mouth opens wide, cracking and splitting, revealing a coiled tongue that drips green saliva.

Genevieve screams.

I don't know what comes over me. I run toward the clown and batter into it like a linebacker. The clown barely budges, but my action catches it by surprise, diverts its attention.

It stands, momentarily releasing Genevieve. It turns its terrifying gaze on me.

"I wanted to save you for last. To savor your fear at the height of my power. But that need not happen . . ."

It lunges toward me, knocking over Grandma's sofa and sending even more knickknacks to the floor. I run out of the way, darting to the other side of the room and wincing at the sound of breaking china.

I know I have to end this. I know I have to be fast, before the clown ends me.

That means getting it back into Grandma's bedroom. But how?

"Victor!" Genevieve calls out. I look over. A second later, she tosses me one of Grandma's knit blankets.

The clown races toward me, and I turn to face it. It roars, so loud my bones ache and the room shakes.

I roar back and run straight for it.

This takes the clown by surprise, just for a moment, just enough time for me to leap in the air with the blanket held high. I net the monster and wrap it tight. Genevieve is right beside me, yanking out more blankets and binding them around the clown. It howls and thrashes.

"This can't hold!" I say.

"It doesn't have to!" she yells back. "Just get it to the bedroom!"

Together, we push the clown down the hallway.

It struggles against us, but we manage together. It's nearly to the door when one of its hands rips out from the blanket and grabs onto my arm.

"If I can't escape, neither will you!" it roars.

I don't know what it means

until Genevieve kicks open the door.

The clown dolls are out of control.

They writhe around the room like ants, clawing and gnashing their teeth.

I know if I step in there, they will tear me apart.

I also know I don't have a choice.

"Victor, you can't," Genevieve says, tears in her eyes.

"I have to," I reply. "Love you, twerp."

Before she can protest, I shove the clown and myself into the bedroom.

The door slams shut behind me, and the next thing I know, my vision darkens as I'm overtaken by clowns.

35

It feels like an eternity of falling, of hearing nothing but the cackling of clowns, feeling nothing but their tiny hands trying to rip me apart, and seeing nothing but darkness as their bodies press the air from my lungs.

Then there is a flash of light, and suddenly the pressure and the cackling are gone.

Moments later, a hand is on my shoulder, helping me sit up.

Shock and confusion muddle my brain. Because the person helping me up is—

"Grandma?"

She smiles down at me, looking stronger and healthier than I've ever seen her.

"In the flesh," she replies.

I glance around.

The clown dolls are all scattered around the room, but they are lifeless. Nothing more than dolls and figurines and tchotchkes.

"What . . . what did you do?" I ask.

"A little magic," she replies with a wink. "I'll teach it to you, someday. You have the spark."

"Wait . . . What?"

Grandma just smiles.

"I still don't understand," I say. "You were sick and in the hospital. How did you . . . ?"

"Mordeth had been draining my power," Grandma says. "When all the clowns were released, he was able to drain more and more. By locking them back in the room, you helped me get my strength and powers back. Just in time too, it seems. It was wise to force Mordeth in here, where he was weak. But without my spell to seal him back into the doll, he would have broken free."

I jolt away from the giant doll at my side, the one that had contained Mordeth. And apparently still does.

"You mean, he isn't gone?"

Grandma shakes her head.

"An evil that strong cannot be defeated. Only contained. So, yes, he is still bound to the doll. But so long as he remains here, he is harmless."

I stare at the doll. It stares back, though its eyes are just glass and its smile just paint.

I want to say it's hard to imagine a great evil lurks inside something so childlike, but it isn't.

I finally understand:

Clowns are terrifying.

Epilogue

"Look sharp, twerp," Sarah says from across the kitchen.

I glance over just in time to see her toss a soda toward me. I manage to catch it, though I nearly fumble it.

"Your reflexes are getting better," her bandmate Alex says. "Maybe someday you can join us in the band."

"Hah! Don't get ahead of yourself," Sarah replies. "Though I bet he'd make a mean drummer."

I smile.

Ever since the event with the clowns, she and I have gotten close. Almost as close as me and Genevieve, who sits on the other side of the kitchen table, doing her homework as always.

"And this one is clearly going to be a lead singer," Alex says, tousling Genevieve's hair. "I bet she's going to be great at screamo."

Genevieve rolls her eyes and doesn't look up from her homework.

Alex comes over and sits next to me. "What are you working on?" she asks.

"History," I reply.

"Eck," she says.

I nod in agreement.

"You two," Sarah says. "Always so studious."

Genevieve shrugs, and Alex starts helping her with her homework. Sarah sidles up next to me. "Have a moment?" she asks.

I nod and stand. She leads me into the living room.

After Grandma came back, Sarah woke up not really remembering much of what had happened.

Honestly, that's probably for the best.

"I wanted to thank you," she says. "For, you know, saving my life."

"I thought you said you couldn't remember?"

"I couldn't," Sarah says. "I think I blocked it out. You know how much clowns scare me. But I talked to Grandma, and she filled me in."

I bite my lip. I hate getting thanked.

"It was nothing," I say.

"It was definitely something," she replies. "I owe you my life. And I'm sorry I didn't believe you earlier."

"It's okay, really," I say. "I'm just glad you're safe."

She pulls me in for an awkward hug. Then she stands up straight.

"I almost forgot!"

She darts off, leaving me standing there and really wishing I could just be doing my homework. Gareth and I have a dungeon to beat, and we're supposed to start in thirty. But I can't play unless homework is done.

"Here," Sarah says, bounding back in the room. "I got you something. A . . . memento. And a thank-you." She hands me a small wrapped parcel, about the size of an avocado.

"You shouldn't have . . . ," I say, unwrapping the gift.

"I found it at the antiques store nearby. It didn't have a price tag, so they gave it to me for free. How cool is that?"

"Pretty sweet," I say.

I freeze when I see what's inside.

A tiny glass clown figurine.

"Isn't it cool?" she asks. "I mean, sorta creepy, but that's the point—to remember what we went through. Together."

I open my mouth, but no words come out. Because yes, it's heartwarming . . .

. . . but I'm also 100 percent certain I'd seen this clown on Grandma's dresser.

I thought we had trapped them all in the house. But if one was out in the world, there were probably others. Others with the soul and power of Mordeth locked inside. Others waiting to escape and cause chaos.

To follow their victims around, scaring them to the very end.

They could be anywhere.

ACKNOWLEDGMENTS

I've never been scared of clowns.

I never had the chance.

I grew up surrounded by larger-than-life clown paintings scattered throughout the house (don't ask me why) so I had to get used to their creepy smiles and glassy eyes. Clowns were everywhere. Which is precisely why I wanted to write this story.

I want to thank everyone at Scholastic for allowing me to write about some of my favorite things, especially my editor David Levithan for his insight and nudging to include even more creepy clown scares. A huge shout-out to Jana Hausmann and the entire Fairs team for their incredible enthusiasm. It's been such a life-changing experience working on these. Thanks to my agent, Brent Taylor, for his continued support. And to my friend and fellow author Will Taylor, for always lending an expert eye.

But mostly, my thanks go to you, dear reader, for loving these creepy tales and always asking for more.

I can't wait to share even more scary stories with you . . . soon.

Just, um, maybe avoid collecting any clown dolls until then.

It might not be safe.